"Let the fever rage, that's the only way."

Calum's voice was deep and sensuous. "Let it run its course and enjoy what it brings. And then, when it burns itself out — well, we each go our own ways, none the worse for the experience. Don't you agree?"

Rissa gasped. Was this how he treated the glamorous society women with whom he was so often photographed?

"Well," he repeated, "do you agree or don't you?"

They stared at each other. Outside the hut, the storm broke in all its fury.

"You feel it too," he murmured persuasively. "Don't you think I can tell? You know as well as I there's only one way to deal with it. So why not make the best of it, Rissa?"

Tormented Rhapsody

Nicola West

HarlequinBooks

TORONTO • NEW YORK • LONDON
AMSTERDAM • PARIS • SYDNEY • HAMBURG
STOCKHOLM • ATHENS • TOKYO • MILAN

Original hardcover edition published in 1984
by Mills & Boon Limited

ISBN 0-373-02669-2

Harlequin Romance first edition January 1985

CHAPTER ONE

'So that's that.' Kate Loring strapped up her last suitcase and looked round the starkly bare room. 'Everything packed up and ready. The end of an era.' She glanced at her two stepdaughters, a faint line of concern on her brow. 'And you're quite happy about it all? Quite sure you're doing the right thing?'

Rissa, the elder of the two, hesitated, but the gap was filled by Mandy, her face alight with impulsive enthusiasm as she assured her stepmother that they were looking forward to the new venture. If only she could feel equally enthusiastic, Rissa thought with an inward sigh. Everything that Mandy said was true—the cottage belonged to them now, they knew the area well and had friends there, and Rissa would certainly be able to cope easily with the cooking involved. In fact, setting up a tea-room had always appealed to her. It wasn't that which bothered her. But nobody else would guess at the cause of her uneasiness, and she wasn't going to tell them.

'You don't have to worry about a thing,' Mandy concluded. 'Just go off to America and enjoy yourself with Alison and all your old friends—and come back as soon as you can to sample one of our teas!'

'I'll need a darn sight more than tea if I've made the journey all the way up to Ichrachan,' Kate responded dryly. 'Motorway or not, it's still a long drive to Scotland.' Rissa, standing by the window and looking out at the park, felt her stepmother's eyes on her. 'You're quiet, Rissa,' the soft American voice went on. 'Not having any doubts, are you?'

If only you knew, Rissa thought wryly, but she turned and smiled. 'No, of course not. Just—well, sorry to be leaving.'

Kate's face softened. 'I know. It's been your home for longer than it's been mine, and I guess it tears at your heart in just the same way.' Her eyes moved over the grave young face, a smooth oval of maturity. 'I guess you had too much responsibility too soon,' she added. 'Losing your own mother when you were only twelve. Sometimes I think you missed a lot of fun, Rissa.'

'Oh no! I didn't miss anything at all.' And Rissa really believed it, not realising that while she'd been acting as a mother to Mandy, five years younger, and almost as a wife to her father, caring for him when he came in from his lectures, listening to talk that was too old and dull for her young ears, her childhood had been slipping by. It had never occurred to her that she herself had no one to turn to, no one in whom to confide her troubles, no one to share her joys. Until Kate had come along eight years ago—and by then it had almost been too late. At fifteen, Rissa had developed a restraint and composure it was difficult to break into, and although she had welcomed Kate as a friend she had never been able to allow her to come any closer. Dimly, she was aware of this; but she had never realised that the answer lay in herself, nor had she realised the strength of the shell she had built around herself.

And what had happened at Ichrachan in that year when Kate and Alison had first joined their family hadn't helped. Already over-sensitive, Rissa had retreated even further into her shell.

'There's the taxi now,' she said. 'I'll take this case, Kate, and you bring the other one and Mandy can manage the odds and ends. What a good job the American airlines go by dimensions rather than weight,' she added, lifting the heavy suitcase. 'Whatever have you got in here, the lead off the church roof?'

'More likely the vicar,' Mandy suggested mischievously. 'Kate always did like him!'

'You two are really dreadful,' Kate scolded, then she paused at the door. 'Just a last look round,' she said softly. 'Like I said, it's the end of an era. We've been a family in this little house; now we're splitting up. I hope——' she glanced with sudden anxiety at the two girls, '—I hope you feel I did a good job.'

They answered her simultaneously, telling her that she'd been wonderful, that they loved her, and finishing with Mandy's sincere: 'The best stepmum anyone ever had!' And then there was a tiny silence, which Rissa broke by saying in her quiet voice: 'You said it yourself when you said we'd been a family. It was the best day in our lives, Kate, when Dad brought you home. And I know you made him happy too.'

There were tears in all their eyes as they recalled the tall, gentle university professor who had meant so much to them all. Since his death three months ago life had been uncertain, as if they had lost direction, as if some essential light had suddenly gone out. Rissa, in particular, had felt lost and alone, drifting rudderless in uncharted seas, and the unexpected loss of her job had made it worse. But now it was time to start again; time for all of them. And as they made their way out of the Georgian house overlooking the park where they had spent so many years, Kate's words echoed in the air. The end of an era . . . the beginning of a new life . . .

What differences would it make to them? Rissa wondered as she helped load their luggage into the taxi. Kate, going to her own daughter in America—herself and Mandy returning to the cottage in Scotland once owned by their mother and left to them in their father's will—how would their lives change? For the better— or . . .?

A sudden inexplicable shiver goosed across her body as she thought of Ichrachan, the tiny village where she had spent so many holidays. It should be—it *was*—full of happy memories. But was it right to go back there— when there was one memory that was far from happy, when to return might be to invite further pain?

Or was she being foolish? Surely by now she ought to have got over what had happened all those years ago;

surely she ought to have forgotten the man who had taken her heart and then left it abandoned as he strode away without a backward glance . . .

'Go to the cottage?' she remembered saying when Mandy had first broached the idea. 'Well, I suppose it would be nice to spend the summer there—but I'm not likely to find a job at Ichrachan, Mandy, and we can't afford to keep it just for our own use. I thought we might try letting it to holidaymakers. It'll have to earn its own keep if we're not to sell it.'

'But that's just what it *will* do,' Mandy had insisted. 'Look, Rissa, this way we'll get the best of both worlds. We'll have the cottage to live in—and it'll earn its own keep, as you say. Yours too—it doesn't matter so much about me, since I'll be getting a university grant.'

Rissa stared at her, her fine brows drawn together. 'I don't know what you're talking about,' she said helplessly. '*How* will it earn its keep? It's not big enough to take in visitors, if that's what you're thinking, there are only three bedrooms——'

'No, I don't mean that.' The small, vivid face was alive with eagerness. 'We could run it as a tea-room, Rissa. There isn't another one for miles, and quite a lot of people go to Ichrachan, you know. It would fill a real need. We could do morning coffees, light lunches, and teas. And with your home baking we might even get into one of those guide books about places to eat. You could probably get someone in from the village to help you when I'm not there, but I'd be able to get it started with you during the summer, and that's the busiest time.' Her brown eyes shone. 'What do you think? Isn't it a good idea? We wouldn't have to give the cottage up, it'd be our home, and you know how you've always loved it there.'

'Yes, I have.' Rissa spoke slowly. The idea of running Cluny Cottage as a tea-room had never occurred to her, but now that Mandy had suggested it she could see its possibilities. Pinching her soft lips thoughtfully between her thumb and forefinger, she got up and moved across the room to look out at the park. *Would* it be possible? And if it were, would it really be such a good idea? There were aspects that Mandy hadn't taken into consideration—either because she didn't know about them, or didn't realise their full significance. Would they affect the situation now, or was Rissa exaggerating their importance?

'It's some years since I went up to Ichrachan,' she said. 'Has—has it changed much?'

'Hardly at all. Why should it? It's not on any main road—the ferry's two miles away at the mouth of the loch. It's just as pretty as ever, and quite a few people do go there to walk or boat, or just to enjoy the scenery. I'm sure a tea-room would do well, Rissa—and it wouldn't hurt to give it a try, would it?' Mandy scrambled up from her favourite position on the floor and came over to her sister. 'I don't want to see strangers in Cluny Cottage,' she murmured persuasively. 'Not even for holidays. It's the only thing of Mother's that we've got.'

Perhaps it was this remark that really decided Rissa. She turned and gave Mandy a quick hug, touched that the younger girl should feel like this about the mother she scarcely remembered. But Cluny Cottage, which had been in their mother's family for generations, had always seemed filled with her presence—even after their father had married Kate Driscoll and taken her and her daughter Alison there to share in the family holidays, that presence had never quite disappeared. And now that both their parents were dead and they were having to leave their home in the south, Cluny really was all that they had left of their childhood.

'All right,' she said. 'We'll think about it—work out what it would involve. And if it seems feasible, we'll try it. After all, I've got to find something to do, and we both need somewhere to live. Cluny's ours, and with my redundancy money we ought to be able to keep ourselves until we can see whether it's going to be a success.'

'It will be, I'm sure it will,' Mandy promised, her young face glowing. 'Oh, I can't wait to get up there and start! Isn't it strange how things work out, Rissa? A few weeks ago it seemed like the end of the world—Dad dying like that and you losing your job when the restaurant closed down. Kate having to sell this house and deciding to go back to America. And now—well, I'm not going to say everything's fine, because it isn't—but at least we can see ahead a little. We're starting a new life, Rissa, and I believe it's going to be a good one!'

'I hope you're right,' Rissa answered soberly, and then, regretting her pessimism, added more warmly: 'I'm *sure* you are.' But she thought of a new life at Ichrachan with a twinge of unease. It had been, for reasons Mandy was unaware of, several years since she had been to Ichrachan. Was it really a good idea to go back? Or would she find that those years had, after all, healed the wound in her heart; that she had become, without knowing it, heartwhole and free?

If that were indeed the case, the sooner she and Mandy returned the better. But she had an uncomfortable feeling that it wasn't going to be quite that easy.

Cluny Cottage had been part of Rissa's life ever since she could remember. With the long holidays that her father's profession of university lecturer had given him, they seemed to have spent months of every summer there, not to mention Easter. At Christmas they had usually stayed at home in the small university town where they still lived; Christmas in Scotland wasn't a big celebration, Rissa's mother had told her, but they must—if the weather was good enough—try to get there for the New Year.

So Rissa's and Mandy's memories were filled with happy times in Scotland, living in the shoreside cottage beside the long sea-loch that stretched a salty finger far inland amongst the wild mountains. Their father had nearly always been busy working in the bedroom

that had been turned into a study—he spent most of the
holidays writing the learned books for which he was
well known—and their mother had occupied much of
her time around the cottage and its small garden,
baking, weeding, making jams and preserves—anything
that would fill the hours usefully until her husband
should want her company, when she was always ready to
stop what she was doing and accompany him on long
walks into the hills.

Mandy had been too small then to be allowed to run
wild as Rissa did. So she hadn't, in those early days,
taken much part in the expeditions that Rissa had
enjoyed with some of the local children—Morag,
daughter of the local innkeeper, who had never been at
a loss for an idea of what to do next; Elspeth, her sister,
always ready to follow where Morag led; Alistair, the
doctor's son, quiet and serious. And Calum.

Even now, Rissa's heart still gave a little bump when
she thought of Calum, and she frowned and scolded
herself for letting it happen—though how you controlled
your heart's behaviour, she still hadn't managed to
fathom. Not that Calum had been a regular member of
their party—he was too old for them, eight years older
than Morag and Alistair, and ten years older than
Rissa. But there was no one of his own age living
around Ichrachan at that time, and his music studies
had kept him isolated. Moreover, he had a sailing
boat—and was willing, now and then, to take them out
in it. He also spent a good deal of time at Cluny
Cottage, for Rissa's mother had given up her own
musical career when she married and took a considerable interest in this solitary boy with his wild black hair
and flashing, steel-grey eyes, and his long, tapering
hands that could wring magic from the keys of any piano.

'He's going to go a long way, is Calum,' Rissa
remembered her telling Professor Loring one day after
Calum had taken himself back to Kilvanie, the lonely
house farther up the loch where he lived with his
grandfather. 'That's if old Mr Kilmartin gives up this idea

of making him go into the family firm and lets him study music properly. A solicitor indeed! Can't he see what talent the boy has?'

'Probably just won't admit it,' Rissa's father answered. 'Remember where that talent comes from— Calum's mother. And the old man never approved of that marriage and has never stopped blaming her for the death of Calum's father.'

'But that's nonsense! They were both killed in that car crash.'

'Yes—but neither would have been if she hadn't persuaded him to take that holiday abroad. Oh, I know you can't reason like that—but old Mr Kilmartin does, solicitor or not. And now he wants Calum to live the life his father would have lived, whether or not he's suited to it. And he won't recognise any likeness to his mother, let alone admit that the boy's probably a musical genius.'

'Crazy,' Mrs Loring had declared. 'Absolutely crazy! But I don't think the old man's going to have it all his own way, you know. Calum's as stubborn as he is—he's certainly inherited *that*. He won't give up without a fight.'

And she'd been right there, Rissa thought. The fight between Calum Kilmartin and his grandfather had raged up and down the glen and had, some said, almost equalled that between the Campbells and the Macdonalds. But in the end, Calum had won. His ultimatum, Rissa's mother had told them, was that unless allowed to go on with his music he would leave Ichrachan for good. And the old man, recognising a will that equalled his own and had the added resilience and strength of youth on its side, had given in. Calum was to go to college to study music. He was to spend as much time as he wished at his piano. Eventually, he had told Mrs Loring, he hoped to become a composer as well as a concert pianist. And she had no doubt that he would.

During this time, Calum had been a regular visitor at

Cluny Cottage. He hadn't taken a lot of notice of Rissa—she was just a small girl then, almost beneath his notice. But it was then that her feelings for him had begun to grow—from the simple adoration of a small girl for one who might have been her elder brother, to the hero-worship of a ten-year-old and, later, the calf-love of a teenager. Although at the time, she had thought it much, much more.

She remembered that summer when she had had her fifteenth birthday. It was the last summer they had spent alone at the cottage, herself and Mandy and their father. They had continued to go there each summer after her mother had died; it was as if only at Ichrachan could the Professor find peace. During the first two summers after his bereavement he had seemed unable to settle to anything, spending long hours roaming the heather-clad hills either with one or both of his daughters, or more often alone. Rissa and Mandy, left to their own devices for much of the time, had gone on in much the same way as before, pottering about the village and harbour with their friends—an enlarged group now, with Mandy and Morag's younger brother Donald joining their expeditions. In some ways little had changed; the six of them drifted in and out of each other's houses, took picnics into the hills, or paddled a fleet of ancient canvas canoes up the loch on the tide, stopping on one of the islands or on the deserted, roadless opposite shore for a barbecue before returning on the outward tide. The same things that they had always done together—but with one big difference; that there was now no gentle mother to welcome the two girls back to Cluny Cottage. And that meant no Calum either. He was home little enough these days, Morag had told Rissa, and when he was, Cluny Cottage, without the woman who had always made time to listen to him and give him the understanding his complex personality needed, seemed to have little attraction.

But during that third summer he had started to come more often. He had been twenty-five then—a well-known concert pianist, with a couple of major prizes already to his credit and a steady list of engagements. A short holiday had brought him back to Ichrachan, he told Rissa, and he seemed glad enough to have her company on his walks or to crew for him in the small sailing-boat he still kept at Kilvanie. And Rissa, still bemused by the magnetism of her childhood hero, had been ready to follow wherever he led.

She remembered in particular one afternoon towards the end of the holiday, when she and Calum had taken food for the day and wandered far into the mountains. They had climbed to over three thousand feet to rest at the peak and look out over the surrounding hills and lochs, identifying the islands that stretched like a rope of green jewels on the shimmering blue silk of the sea, and picking out the lochs that lay like patches of fallen sky amongst the cloud-dappled mountains. Then they unpacked and ate their lunch, resting their backs against sun-warmed rocks and idly scanning the skies for a glimpse of the golden eagle that was often to be seen hunting amongst the crags.

Calum finished his sandwiches and stretched out on his back, closing his eyes against the sunshine. Rissa watched him, studying his face almost as if she were learning it—almost as if she expected never to see him again and needed to impress every detail on her memory. She let her eyes travel over his face, craggy now with rough dark brows that gave him a fierce, impatient look, framed in the black hair that had never been tamed. Those eyes, when open, would be the piercing grey of finely-honed steel; the firm mouth could break into a smile that was devastatingly attractive, revealing teeth as white and strong as the snow-capped mountain peaks in the depths of winter. His body, outlined under the thin T-shirt and shorts that he wore for walking, was powerfully built and muscular; he had told her once that a pianist's job was physically demanding and he had to keep fit to be able to cope with the demands of playing, for instance, a long concerto, let alone the hours of practice he must put in each day. She looked at the muscles of his arms, firmed by his position as he lay with his hands under the back of his head; at the depth of his chest narrowing to a flat stomach, and the strong length of his thighs and calves.

'How much?' His voice broke in on her thoughts and she jerked her topaz eyes back to his face, colouring guiltily as she caught the mocking glance and realised that he must have seen her staring at him.

'I—I don't understand——' she floundered, and Calum's smile widened, showing strong white teeth.

'You were looking at me as a butcher might assess a prize steer. I just wondered how much a pound you thought I was worth.'

'No—I wasn't—I mean, I never thought——' For the first time, Rissa found herself feeling disconcerted, even angry with Calum. She was at a loss and she didn't properly understand herself, let alone him. In fact, she had an uneasy feeling that *he* probably understood her all too well, and it was a feeling she didn't much like. She bit her lip and looked away, feeling the scarlet colour flame through her cheeks. Somehow in the last few moments their easy relationship had changed, and suddenly she didn't know how to cope.

Calum sat up and studied her. His craggy face was serious now, but when Rissa glanced back at him she felt sure that there was a twinkle somewhere in those sea-grey eyes. Amusement? Mockery? Scorn? More uncomfortable than ever, she began to gather their picnic things together and pack them into the rucksack. A cloud passed across the sun, and in the sudden chill she felt as if a shadow had crossed her life.

'Don't be upset,' Calum said gently. 'It comes to us all, you know. I just wonder why I never realised it before.'

'Realised what?' she jerked out. 'I—I don't know what you mean.'

'Don't you?' He considered her. 'No, maybe you

don't. But I think you soon will, Rissa. And it's really nothing to worry about. We all have to start somewhere.'

Rissa stared at him, bewildered and unaccountably near to tears. Vaguely, she knew that somewhere in the recesses of her mind she understood him—but she didn't want to pull the understanding out into daylight and look at it. *No*, her mind shouted, *it's too soon. Not yet—not yet*. But something else was urging her on—telling her it wasn't too soon, that now was the time, that if she missed this chance it would never come again ... And between the two she was caught without any real comprehension of the conflict that raged within her; caught here on a mountain-top, with nowhere to run to. ...

Calum reached out and touched her chin with a strong forefinger, lifting it gently so that she was forced to meet his eyes. He stared at her, his eyes knifing into her mind so that she longed to look away, to cut short the communication that seemed to exist between them without any volition of hers; but Calum's finger kept her there and she was helpless even to close her own eyes against that needle-sharp scrutiny.

Calum bent nearer and his lips brushed hers, gently, passionlessly. Rissa's eyes closed. She remained quite still, conscious only of the tenderness of the finely-chiselled lips against hers and the wild pounding of her heart. Then Calum withdrew and she opened dazed, honey-coloured eyes that searched his face and asked questions she scarcely understood.

'Don't worry, little Rissa,' he said at last, his voice soft. 'I'm not going to hurt you.' A short pause, then he added in a different tone: 'How old are you?'

'Fifteen,' she whispered, miserably aware of the gap between them, a gap of ten long years. 'I—I'll be sixteen in September.'

'September,' he murmured. 'Well, I'll be gone then.' His voice was suddenly brisk as he took his hand away, and Rissa felt suddenly cold, as if someone had removed a warm coat from her shoulders.

'Gone?' she repeated. 'I—I didn't know. Where are you going?'

'Back to work, of course.' His voice was amused again and she cursed herself for being so young, so gauche. 'I'm playing at the Edinburgh Festival and then doing some engagements on the Continent. So I'm afraid I shan't be seeing you again for a while.' He came lithely to his feet and took the rucksack, swinging it easily on to his broad shoulders. 'But I'll be back next year. I've decided that a break in my home surroundings is an essential if I'm to retain my sanity for the rest of the year! What about you?'

'Me?' Rissa blinked.

'Yes—will you be here as usual next year?'

'Oh—yes. Yes, I'm sure we will.' I'll *make* sure of it, she thought, gazing up at him with shining eyes, hardly able to believe that he was saying what she thought he was saying—asking what she longed for him to ask. 'Yes, we'll be here, just as usual.'

Calum looked down at her and then he touched her cheek with that same forefinger. 'That's fine,' was all he said; but as Rissa followed him down the rough mountain track she felt a soaring happiness, even though she was already wondering just how she was ever going to get through the next twelve months.

Anyway, I'll have had time to grow up by then, she thought as she picked her way along in his wake. I won't be a stupid, blushing schoolgirl any more. I'll be a woman.

But although she had certainly grown up quite a lot before she saw Calum Kilmartin again, there had been other changes too. By Christmas, Professor Loring had met and married Kate Driscoll, the American widow of one of his friends from undergraduate days. And when the family next came up to Cluny Cottage the party included both Kate and her daughter Alison, although for Kate it wasn't a first visit, Professor Loring having brought her here during the Easter holidays.

Rissa knew as soon as she met Alison that here was the kind of girl she dreamed of becoming. Tall, slim but voluptuous, with long blonde hair and cornflower-blue eyes, it was easy to see why the older girl had made such a success of her career of modelling. Now she was taking a break, a year's holiday to see Britain and some of Europe before returning to America to continue her career. To Rissa and Mandy, she was like a being from some other, exotic world. And when they went to Scotland for their customary visit, she stood out like a jewelled butterfly on rough tweed.

During that year Rissa had heard nothing from Calum. She had followed his career whenever she could get news of him and knew that he had played brilliantly at Edinburgh and at the Festival Hall in London, following these successes with a tour of the Continent. But the excitement and upheaval of her father's marriage had made it difficult to concentrate on anything else. Kate's moving into the Georgian house had brought its own joys and difficulties—luckily, both girls liked their new stepmother and were only too pleased to see their father happy once more, but there were inevitable adjustments to be made. And on top of everything else, Rissa was working hard for her summer examinations at school.

Nevertheless, she kept Calum very much in her mind and relived that afternoon on the mountain many times as she lay in bed at night, conjuring up Calum's face, recalling how she had studied him as he lay with eyes closed; going over and over every word he had said and convincing herself of the hidden meaning that she was sure lay behind his words.

He would be there in the summer, she knew. And once again they would walk on the hills, climb the mountains, sail to the lonely shore opposite Ichrachan. And now that she was a woman—almost seventeen— perhaps Calum would tell her what was in his heart. . . .

But her thoughts weren't always so hopeful. Sometimes they grew frighteningly realistic. Calum was an attractive man, she would tell herself, a man ten years older than herself, a virile man who couldn't be expected to live the life of a monk. He must meet many women on these tours; glamorous women who knew his world and moved about it with ease and confidence. Women of poise and experience. . . . She would think again of that powerful body and wonder about the women he met, wonder if he ever gave even a passing thought to the leggy teenager he had known by the lochside. . . .

And when, at last, they were on their way up to Scotland for the longed-for holiday, she looked at Alison, who was so exactly the kind of woman she had envisaged Calum as escorting round the capitals of Europe, and wondered why she had ever thought that she might have a chance.

'And you really mean to say he might be around?' Alison drawled in her attractive American voice, as Mandy's chatter broke across Rissa's thoughts. 'Rissa, this sister of yours tells me you have a famous neighbour up in the Highlands. Calum Kilmartin, the pianist, is that right? Do you really mean to say you know him?'

'Oh yes,' Rissa confirmed. 'We've known Calum all our lives. Of course, he doesn't come home so often now, especially since his grandfather died. Old Mr Kilmartin was his only relative, apart from a sister who moved up to Fort William when she married. But he was there last year for a few weeks.'

'But he said he'd be coming back this year, didn't he?' Mandy chimed in. 'You told me that, Rissa.'

'He said he *might*,' Rissa corrected her, choosing to forget that Calum had been quite definite about it. 'It depends on his engagements.'

'Well, let's hope he does, then,' Alison remarked. 'From what you've told me there's going to be precious little company up there apart from the stags and the fishermen! It'll wake the place up a bit to have an attractive man about the place. And is Calum Kilmartin

attractive! If his photos are anything to go by, he's
God's gift to womankind!'

Rissa listened silently. There was no reason why
Alison shouldn't talk like this—she was lively and
beautiful and she enjoyed the company of attractive
men. Already Rissa had realised that Alison was the
type of girl to have a bevy of admirers, without letting
any of them get too serious—'safety in numbers', she
had remarked once with a laugh. And it was perfectly
clear that she wouldn't only be attracted by Calum, she
would almost certainly attract him too. There didn't
seem to be much that Rissa could do about it. Except
hope that his words last year really had meant
something. And the more she thought about them now,
the less likely that seemed.

But Calum wasn't at Kilvanie when they arrived at
Cluny Cottage. He hadn't been there yet, Donald Gill
told them when he called on their first morning there to
see that they had everything they wanted. And nobody
had heard whether he was coming or not.

'But you know Calum,' he added, a grin on his
friendly, freckled face. 'Comes and goes just as he feels.
And why shouldn't he? Now that the old man's gone
there's no one here he needs to tell.'

Donald was almost thirteen then, a sturdy lad with
curly red hair and honest blue eyes. Rissa found herself
liking him as much as she had his sisters, and nodded at
Kate when Donald asked if any of them would like to
go out fishing in the boat belonging to the inn. Only
Mandy was likely to want to go, she knew, but she
would be safe enough with Donald.

And that left herself and Alison more or less thrown
together. Professor Loring, although not writing a book
during these holidays, was just as absorbed in his new
wife and they looked like treating this holiday as an
extended honeymoon. By common consent, the two
stepsisters left them to it and went off on expeditions of
their own, often using the car since Alison was no
walker, but occasionally leaving it to explore some of

the picturesque valley paths, wandering beside tumbling streams and lazing in the heather.

And it was on one of these days, when the sun beat down out of a hot blue sky and a raven coughed somewhere amongst the windswept rowans, they that met Calum.

Alison saw him first. She was sitting up, arms linked loosely round her knees, long blonde hair flowing down her slim shoulders like a pale cascade of gold, gazing reflectively at the hurrying water. Rissa was lying on her back, eyes closed, absorbed in the rainbow of colour behind her lids. She had almost drifted off to sleep when she heard Alison's soft voice.

'My, oh, my! And is this the Monarch of the Glen? Or is it—Rissa, sit up! I'm sure it's your local genius— tell me if I'm right, for goodness' sake!'

Rissa opened her eyes, blinking against the light, and sat up. She glanced over the stream to where Alison was pointing; and her heart kicked.

'Yes,' she murmured tonelessly. 'Yes, that's Calum.' And she hoped that Alison wouldn't look at her then; wouldn't see the betraying colour that had swept into her cheeks, leaving her hot and flustered.

Calum was coming down the hillside opposite at a fairly fast pace. Obviously, he still believed in keeping fit; he looked as if he spent all his life on the open mountain, instead of mostly indoors sitting at a piano. He was wearing the shorts he favoured for walking, and his legs looked hard and tanned even at this distance, the muscles firm as he leapt lightly down the rocks. His shirt was unbuttoned almost to the waist and the dark curling hairs were clearly visible, along with the thin gold medallion he had worn ever since Rissa could remember. As the two girls watched, he glanced over and saw them, gave a wave of his hand and changed direction so that he would reach the spot where they were sitting.

'So that's the musical genius,' Alison breathed. 'Well, well! He certainly lives up to his photos. And you say he isn't married?'

'Not as far as I know,' Rissa answered, trying to keep her voice casual but wondering with a sickening lurch of the heart whether she *would* know if Calum had married since last year. Oh, surely she would! Someone in Ichrachan would have heard. But there was always the chance. It could have been kept quiet. And this new anxiety gnawed agonisingly at her mind as she waited for Calum to reach them.

'Hi! If it isn't young Rissa—welcome back to the glen!' His grey eyes swept over her, then turned to Alison, and Rissa saw them sharpen with interest. 'And who's this? I've not seen you around Ichrachan before.'

'You certainly haven't,' Alison laughed at him, and Rissa said:

'This is my new sister, Alison Driscoll. You've heard Daddy's got married again, I expect?'

'Yes, but not until the other day.' Calum's eyes were frankly admiring as he looked at Alison. 'Well, what an addition to the community! And so young Rissa's showing you around, is she?'

Rissa wished he could say her name without the tag of *young* every time. It seemed to put her firmly into her place—into a different generation from himself, and Alison—and she didn't like it. But there was nothing to be done. She had known from the start what his reaction was likely to be on seeing her stepsister. And she had to admit that Alison, even wearing jeans and a T-shirt, was still a glamorous and exotic sight. While Rissa was acutely conscious of being—still—nothing more than the leggy teenager he had known last year, and not glamorous at all.

'When did you arrive, Calum?' she enquired, not wanting to lose her part in the conversation, for from the way Calum and Alison were looking at each other it seemed likely.

'Oh, yesterday,' he answered vaguely. 'I've had a pretty strenuous tour and I suddenly felt I needed a bit of time to myself. So as I haven't anything fixed for the next couple of weeks, Kilvanie seemed the best place to be.' He turned to Alison. 'And you certainly seem to have brought good weather with you. Where are you from? Surely that's an American accent.'

The two of them laughed and chatted while Rissa sat silent, her heart sinking even further. So Calum had forgotten his words of the previous year. He'd probably never given them a thought, dismissed from his mind the half-promise he'd made her. Her head drooped and the sunlight seemed to dim. He had asked her her age, as if it was important. But it hadn't been. She wasn't important to him at all, and never could be. Not while there were women like Alison around, lively and beautiful, able to talk with him on his own level. They were discussing America now—Calum had been there two years ago and they were comparing notes. Next, it would be the Continent, where Alison had already made several visits. How could Rissa compete with that kind of thing? She had been abroad once, on a school trip to France. Neither of her companions were likely to want to hear about *that*.

It was the same as they made their way back down the valley to Ichrachan. Calum and Alison walked ahead, totally absorbed in each other, while Rissa followed, all but forgotten. And she couldn't even work up any anger about it. They weren't deliberately ignoring her—every now and then one of them— usually Alison—would turn and try to draw her into the conversation. But Rissa's mind was dulled and she could think of only monosyllabic answers. And after a while they gave up.

'Honey, what was the matter with you?' Alison asked later. 'Don't you like Calum?'

'Yes, he's all right,' Rissa answered offhandedly. 'We just don't have much in common, that's all. He's a lot older than me—sees me as a kid, I suppose.'

'Hm.' Alison looked at her thoughtfully. 'Well, that's a pity, because I'd like to see more of him. In fact, he's asked me to go off on one or two trips with him, but I don't like to leave you on your own.'

'Oh, you needn't worry about that,' Rissa said lightly, her heart burning. 'I can go with Mandy and Donald if I want to, and I think Morag will be home next week—she's been away helping an aunt who's been ill. You go and enjoy yourself with Calum, Alison. I'll be all right.'

'Well, so long as you're sure,' the American girl said. 'I wouldn't want to spoil your holiday.'

Rissa turned away. She wanted to say 'no chance of that', but the lie was too big. Her holiday was already spoilt. And, being Rissa, she wanted desperately to keep that fact to herself. Rissa's feelings were private; she didn't like to let anyone know when she was hurt.

'I told you, you go with Calum.' Her voice was brittle and she could only hope that Alison hadn't noticed. 'I'll be quite happy.'

And Alison had gone with Calum. The next day, the day after that, and every day, until it was obvious that they were head over heels in love. They became inseparable. Wherever one was, you could be sure of finding the other, either at Cluny Cottage or at Kilvanie, sailing in Calum's boat—though Alison preferred to use the engine—or wandering in the valleys that ran up from the lochside into the heathery folds of the hills. Or setting off in Calum's BMW to go heaven knew where, returning late at night when the rest of Ichrachan was fast asleep.

'Do you think Alison and Calum are going to get married?' Mandy asked one day as she and Rissa made sandwiches for their own day out.

Rissa hesitated, feeling the shaft of despair in her heart as Mandy voiced a possibility she hadn't been willing to face. 'I don't know,' she said lamely, but Mandy went on.

'They seem awfully in love, don't they? And it was *three o'clock* this morning before Alison came home. I should think they'll have to get married soon, won't they?'

Rissa stopped what she was doing and stared at her young sister. 'What on earth do you mean?'

'Well, people do, don't they? When they're in love.'
Mandy licked some crab spread off her fingers,
oblivious of Rissa's reaction. 'D'you think Alison will
have me as bridesmaid?'

'I've no idea,' Rissa answered shortly. 'And I don't
think it's a good idea for you to wonder about it like
that. They might not like it.' Any more than I do, she
added silently. And saw, reluctantly, a picture of Calum
and Alison coming side by side out of the little kirk at
Ichrachan; arm in arm, smiling and happy. The spear of
despair twisted in her heart. I won't be able to bear it,
she thought. I just won't!

But as it happened, she hadn't been expected to bear
it. Because Calum and Alison hadn't married. At the
end of the holiday, Alison had returned to Cluny
Cottage alone, with a face like ashes. In a flat, toneless
voice, she had told them that Calum had gone away,
and that she didn't expect to see him again.

Nothing had been the same after that. Alison had left
Scotland and gone on with her trip to the Continent.
And Rissa, who should have been relieved at the news,
found instead that she was furiously angry with the
man who had hurt her stepsister so badly. The love that
she had felt for him turned to hate. She too felt that she
never wanted to see him again—this man whom they
called a genius and who took his pleasure by raising the
hopes of the women who loved him and then dashing
them cruelly to the ground. He had done it to her, he
had done it to Alison. How many other women had he
made suffer in the same sadistic way?

She had been glad when her training in hotel work
and catering had kept her too busy to visit Cluny for
the next few years. And now, when she and Mandy
were on the point of returning to make it their home, a
tingle of unease kept touching her spine. Was she being
wise to go? Or was she simply asking for the old
wounds to be re-opened—for the old pain to start
again?

CHAPTER TWO

'YOU'RE right, Mandy. It hasn't changed a bit.'

Rissa climbed out of the small estate car she had bought and stood gazing around. The breeze that blew off the loch whipped her soft hair into curls and brought colour to her cheeks. She looked up and down the shore, picking out features that had been familiar to her all her life, automatically identifying the great shoulders of the mountains that surrounded the loch, their peaks lost in the scudding clouds. The shadows of those same clouds raced across hillside and water, patterning the landscape with ever-changing movement, deepening the colour of the amethyst slopes with the shades of purple that would come later when the heather was in full bloom.

Nearer at hand the tiny village of Ichrachan seemed to slumber in the late afternoon sun. A few boats danced on the sparkling water of the little harbour. An old man sat smoking a pipe on a bollard. A few hens wandered across the deserted road and an old spaniel lay dozing in the warmth.

Nothing there had changed. And neither had Cluny Cottage. It still stood, white and gay with flowers, a little apart from the rest of the village, its garden sloping gently to the water's edge. We'll be able to put chairs and tables out there for fine days, Rissa thought. With umbrellas. She and Mandy had already earmarked the large parlour for their tea-room. It would be possible, they had calculated, to seat about sixteen people in there, at small tables for four. It would be a little crowded, but any less wouldn't be economical. 'And we're not likely to be full all the time,' Rissa had remarked, only to be taken severely to task by Mandy, who was determined that their tea-room should be the talk of the Highlands.

'Your baking will be a byword,' she prophesied. 'You'll have to make lots of scones—and shortbread—and flapjacks. And some of your specials—apricot loaf, fudge slices and whisky cake. That'll bring them in!'

'And I can see just where I'll be spending most of *my* time,' Rissa commented ruefully. 'Still, that big freezer we've ordered should help. And we'll only be doing light lunches.'

'Home-made soups, pâté and fresh rolls and baps,' Mandy agreed. 'With a selection of cheeses, of course. Oh, and some of those delicious sweets you make—*nobody* could resist that chocolate chestnut pie, or your gorgeous hazelnut meringue, or that lovely light lemon cream gateau, or——'

'Stop!' Rissa protested, laughing. 'I'll never be able to make all those by myself. You'll have to learn to cook too, Mandy!'

'You must be joking,' her sister retorted, and Rissa had to agree. Mandy's culinary experiments had so far been little short of disastrous.

'All right. I'll do my best, and you'll have to charm the customers into eating it all. And help with the washing-up,' she added, and Mandy made a face. But Rissa knew that there would be no shirking whatever had to be done. Mandy was, for some reason, even more keen than she that the Cluny Cottage tea-room should be a success, and if enthusiasm were all that was needed, there ought to be no doubt about it.

And now here they were. Everything had been ordered; the new freezer without which Rissa dared not face the mountain of cooking she would have to tackle before they could even open, was to be installed tomorrow. They could then make a trip into Oban to stock up with all the ingredients they would need before she could start, and while she was baking Mandy and Donald would be redecorating the parlour and fitting it out with the furniture and bric-à-brac they were bringing up from the south to give a cosy, homely atmosphere to their tea-room.

'It's lovely to be back, isn't it?' Mandy said softly, getting out of the car to join Rissa. 'I don't think I'm ever going to want to go away again.'

'Well, you'll have to,' Rissa reminded her. 'You go to university in October, remember?'

'Mm.' But Mandy didn't seem to want to follow up that remark. She wandered down to the shore and stretched as if she were embracing the entire landscape, loch, mountains and all. Then she turned and came back to Rissa and her introspective mood seemed to have passed, leaving her face as vivid and lively as ever. 'Come on!' she cried, tugging a case out of the car and setting off up the path. 'Let's get unpacked. Let's get *started*!'

It took quite a while to get all their luggage out of the car and sorted out. Mandy had insisted that Rissa have the largest bedroom, the one their parents and, more recently, their father and stepmother, had occupied. 'You'll be living here all the time,' she said, leading Rissa into the room overlooking the loch and dumping her case squarely in the middle of it. 'And I've always loved my little room next door. It has the same view, so you won't be depriving me!'

Fortunately there was sufficient furniture in the cottage, except for the extra chairs and tables needed for the tea-room. In fact there was almost too much; to use the third bedroom for storage they had to push the bed against the wall and squash the small chest of drawers and wardrobe together in a corner. They spent the next few hours getting straight: and then Rissa declared a halt and suggested a walk along the shore before bed.

'Well, actually I thought I'd go down to the village and see if Donald's around,' Mandy admitted. 'Do you mind, Rissa? I want to give him his orders if he's going to help with the redecorating!'

'Poor Donald,' Rissa smiled. 'I wonder if he realises what he's let himself in for. All right, Mandy, you go. I don't mind walking alone. See you later.'

She watched the slight figure of her sister, with her almost black hair bouncing around her head, running eagerly towards the village. The friendship with Donald seemed to have lasted through the years, even though both had grown up. He had just finished at university, Mandy had told her, and Rissa wondered what he would do next. Donald was a bright boy and should go quite a long way. She wondered too about the rest of their little group—Elspeth, Morag and Alistair. They all seemed to have left the village now. Alistair, she knew, had recently finished at medical school and was working as a houseman in a Glasgow hospital. She hoped he would come back to Ichrachan soon—it would be nice to see Alistair's pleasant, homely face again. He and she had always been good friends.

The cottage was quiet without Mandy. It was strange to be here, just the two of them. It had always been such a family place. Now it belonged equally to her and Mandy and was to be their permanent home. She hoped it would work out.

Rissa stepped out into the cool evening air and closed the door softly behind her. A milky dusk lay over the loch, a dusk that would last for several hours yet; at this time of year it never got properly dark. She went down to the shore and turned to follow it inland, breathing in the clear salty air and listening to the sounds of the birds settling down for the night. Tiny wavelets lapped the shingle as she walked, and for the first time for months she felt at peace.

And then her tranquil mood was shattered. As she paused to look out across the water, watching the silver-green ripples in the hope of seeing the surface broken by the dark round head of a seal, she heard footsteps crunch along the shingle towards her. And when she turned her head it was almost with a feeling of inevitability; as if she had known all along that somewhere along these shores she would meet again the man who had awoken her heart seven years ago, and then left it cold.

'Hallo, Calum,' she said, her voice cool and even.

Calum Kilmartin came down the shore and stood beside her. He was even bigger than she remembered, square and powerful in the twilight, so tall that she had to tilt her head back to look up at him. He had aged too, she noticed; the face was craggier than ever, a dusting of grey in the shaggy brows, a touch of silver in the black hair at his temples. Not that it made him any the less attractive; if anything he was ever more disturbing. He was thirty-three now, in the prime of life. Yet she had still never heard that he had married or even heard his name linked with any woman, in any serious sense. He was often photographed with beautiful girls, but there was never any suggestion that one might become a permanent feature in his life.

Calum looked down at her and she caught her breath as the bright grey glance met hers, as sharp as ever. There was no smile to break the sternness of his face, no movement of his muscles to show he was pleased to see her, and a feeling of resentment grew in her heart. Couldn't he at least show her some kind of welcome after all these years?

'So you're back.' His voice was flat.

'The same old perceptive Calum, I see,' Rissa returned, and saw his mouth tighten. She wondered wildly what had happened. She'd never spoken to Calum like this—never wanted to. But he had never approached her with that cold hostility before; he had always treated her with the easy familiarity of an elder brother. Until that summer when he had kissed her. . . She had sensed a new tenderness in him then, but it hadn't lasted—not once he had seen Alison.

The memory of the way he had treated Alison made sense of it. Rissa's own feelings towards him had changed then, hadn't they—when she saw him for what he was, a cold-hearted philanderer. She hadn't seen Calum after that, but she could guess that his own hostility stemmed from that time too. A guilty conscience—or did he just not think about it any more?

'I was sorry to hear about your father,' he said after a pause. 'Kate's gone back to America, has she?'

'Yes, she's gone to see Alison. I don't know if she intends to stay there for good—she'll come back to this country first anyway.'

'And Alison?' His voice was casual. 'Still modelling?'

'Yes. She may be thinking of getting married, though, from what Kate says.'

'Alison? Married?' He gave a short laugh. 'Guess the guy must be rich!'

His fake American accent annoyed Rissa, who said sharply: 'I've no idea. I imagine she must love him. That's the usual reason for getting married, isn't it?'

'Is it? I wouldn't know, never having tried the holy trap.'

'That's a cynical thing to say,' said Rissa. She looked up at him. 'You've changed, Calum. You used to be a pleasant, easy, friendly person. And now——'

'Now I'm not. You don't really have to tell me that, Rissa. I'm all too well aware of it.' Bitterness twisted the mobile mouth. 'Let's not discuss me—it's a boring subject. Tell me about yourself. Married? Or maybe you follow the fashion and just shack up for a while——'

'No, I don't!' Calum's sour tones angered her. 'I haven't even thought about marriage yet—or any other relationship. I'm quite happy living my own life, thank you!'

'And that is?' Not that he sounded interested, but she might as well tell him.

'Since I left school I've trained in hotel management and done a catering course. I worked at a hotel in London and then moved to a bistro near home. Unfortunately it had to close down a couple of months ago, just after my father died, so Mandy and I have come up here. We're going to run Cluny as a tea-room.'

'A *tea-room*? *Cluny*?' Calum's eyes flashed in the dim light as he turned to her. 'You're not serious!'

'Yes, we are. Why shouldn't we be? And what's it got to do with you, anyway?' Rissa wished this new, strange

Calum would go away. He was so different from the Calum she had known, and the change in him was heartbreaking.

'Why shouldn't you?' he repeated. 'You'll only change Ichrachan beyond recognition, that's all. Bring hordes of sightseers and tourists to mill around the place and drop litter and play their transistor radios. My God, and I thought it was the one haven of peace left to mankind! I was wrong. There aren't any.'

'Oh, don't be so ridiculous! We're starting a tea-room, not a safari park. People come to Ichrachan anyway, and it won't do any harm to offer them a cup of tea. All right, maybe a few more will come if we advertise a bit and make ourselves known—but would that be so very terrible?'

'Yes, it would,' he flashed back. 'I come here for peace and quiet and I don't want the thronging hordes spoiling it. You say you're only starting a tea-room, but you know as well as I do how that kind of thing can grow. Next thing there'll be a craft shop and a yachting marina and God knows what else, and Ichrachan will be spoilt for ever.'

'You're exaggerating,' Rissa told him wearily. 'And I find your attitude totally hypocritical. You don't mind the crowds when they're paying to come and listen to you, I presume. Though why they should want to is beyond my understanding.'

Calum raised his thick brows, his eyes glimmering. 'You don't enjoy my music?'

'Not the kind of thing you've been playing lately, no,' she retorted boldly. 'I like music to have some sense in it—a melody, a tune. Not be just a jangle of noise that goes nowhere and says nothing.'

'You don't enjoy any modern music?' he pursued.

'Not much, no.'

'And for that you blame the composer and the musicians who interpret his work? You don't blame yourself at all?'

'Why should I? Why should I even think about it?

There's plenty of music about that I do enjoy. Tchaikovsky—Rimsky-Korsakov——'

'Sugar is more to your liking than savoury, in fact,' he said smoothly.

'Oh, I don't know what you're talking about,' Rissa declared crossly. 'You used to play Tchaikovsky and the rest yourself. Now it's all modern stuff, and you're adding to the jangle with your own compositions. And we're supposed to *like* them! Why?'

Calum shrugged. 'It's just a matter of knowing how to listen. Just as modern art is a matter of knowing how to look. And if you can extend your range, derive more pleasure from a wider scope, why not?'

Rissa felt suddenly helpless. She had no idea how they had got into this argument and she didn't want it to continue. Calum was intent on scoring over her, she knew that. And, dimly, she knew that this argument had nothing to do with music. It was operating on some deeper level, a deeper level than she fully understood. Even if she wanted to.

'I'm going back to Cluny Cottage now,' she said, interrupting a flow of words she hadn't even heard. 'It's been nice meeting you again, Calum. I hope you have a good holiday. And since we don't expect to open for another week, at least you've got that much peace and quiet left before the madding crowds arrive to ruin it.'

She turned away, intending to leave him there, too tired now to bother with any more argument. But she hadn't gone two steps before she felt a hand on her shoulder; a big, powerful hand with long fingers that gripped cruelly and twisted her back to face him. Suddenly angry, she glared up at him, her hazel eyes fiery and the colour in her cheeks like flags of war.

'Let me go!' she blazed. 'What do you think you're doing? Let *go*!'

'Not until you've told me what's eating you.' Calum gave her shoulder a shake. 'What's happened to the Rissa I knew? You tell me *I've* changed—but so have you, you know! You never used to be a spitting little virago, taking offence at every little thing. What's got into you—some man, is it, who's hurt your pride so that you take it out on the rest of us? What happened—couldn't you give him what he wanted? Is that why *you* haven't thought about marriage?'

Rissa gasped. She could scarcely believe her ears. Could this really be the Calum she had spent so many happy hours with in the past, the Calum she had loved since childhood? This bitter man, his mouth twisted with scorn? But he had gone too far this time, and she wrenched violently away from him before swinging her hand hard against his cheek in a slap that could have been heard on the far side of the loch.

'Don't you dare talk to me like that!' she panted, too furious to consider the consequences of her action. 'Just because the world hasn't turned out to be your oyster after all—although why you should think that, I just can't begin to understand. You're a successful musician, you're starting to get known as a composer, you go all over the world, meet all kinds of people—yet you're still not satisfied. Well, let me tell you this, Calum Kilmartin—there's nothing eating *me*, but there seems to be a hell of a lot eating *you*, and my advice to you is to get yourself sorted out. There are people who do that sort of thing, and you ought to be able to afford the best!'

She turned away then, but just not quickly enough. Once again Calum's hands descended on her shoulders, twisting her to face him. And then she was trapped by arms that felt like steel bands, pulling close against a body that was as rigid as living rock, and when she looked up, her mouth open to protest, she caught only a glimpse of the fire in his eyes before his lips came down on hers, blotting out everything else as they bruised and plundered her soft mouth. Taken completely by surprise, she remained passive for a few moments, shaken by the probing intimacy of the kiss, her senses reeling as without her volition her body began to respond, her heart thundering against his chest, her legs trembling so that she was forced to cling to him to remain standing, her hands finding their own way up into his hair to tangle there and hold him even closer against her.

And then, for a brief flash of seconds, common sense returned and she struggled in panic, trying frantically to pull her head away from his, push his body away from hers. Her cries became whimpers, her struggles only brought them into even closer contact, and she was blindingly aware of the virility of the body pressing so hard against hers. So aware that common sense faded again and to her own astonishment she allowed herself to relax against him, her body melting to his contours which in turn became more flexible against her. His lips, so hard and cruel, became more tender, playing with her mouth in a way that had her trembling in his arms, and then leaving to trail a burning path of kisses down the line of her cheek and neck to the top button of her open-necked shirt.

When he let her go at last, she staggered and had to hold him while she regained balance. Still quivering, she looked up at him, dazed and bewildered by what had happened. Was he mocking her? She could have sworn that the kiss had started out as a punishment— but something had happened to it along the way, and she wasn't at all sure she wanted to analyse what it was. But she knew that if Calum laughed at her now, she wouldn't be able to bear it.

But he wasn't laughing. He was staring down at her, a strange light in his eyes. For a moment, the bitterness was gone and his face was once again the face of the young Calum, the Calum she had laughed with and loved. And then his expression closed again and he turned away, as if unable to bear the sight of her any longer.

'I'm sorry about that, Rissa,' he said, and his voice was harsh. 'Perhaps we'd better pretend it never happened. And I'll make a bargain with you. You stay at Cluny Cottage and I'll stay at Kilvanie. That way it'll be best for both of us.'

He was gone, tramping away along the shingled

shoreline, and Rissa watched him, confused and troubled. There was something here she didn't understand. Something that went very, very deep.

'There!' Mandy set the last chair in place and stood back to admire the effect. 'Doesn't it look lovely!'

Rissa came in from the kitchen and the three of them crowded in the doorway. The ex-parlour, now the tea-room, was transformed. Gone were the whitewashed walls, the plain curtains and the shabby but comfortable furniture that had made the parlour an easy, undemanding room to live in. In their place were a pretty, fresh wallpaper with a design of small green flowers on a white background, a hard-wearing moss-green carpet and pale sprigged curtains. On the walls were a few pictures of local scenes, mostly watercolours done by an artist who was pleased to have somewhere to display her work, and on the windowsill and mantelpiece stood jugs of fresh flowers and grasses picked near the cottage. There were four small round tables, each with four chairs tucked neatly underneath, covered with circular cloths that matched the curtains. The whole effect was light, pretty and welcoming, and Rissa turned to congratulate the two decorators who had worked so hard.

'Well, you've been hard at it too,' said Mandy. 'Actually, it hasn't made our job any easier, has it, Donald, having to sniff at all those enticing smells that keep wafting out from the kitchen. If you hadn't given us a sample with our tea and coffee-breaks you'd have had a strike on your hands!'

'Too true,' Donald agreed. 'And if I've any influence at all round these parts the tourists won't be able to get inside the door. I've been praising your cooking all round the village!'

'Well, let's hope you're right,' said Rissa, feeling nervous now that opening day was so close. 'Mandy, are you sure there's nothing I've forgotten? It would be awful to find we haven't got something so basic neither of us has thought of it!' She moved to the window. 'The tables look very nice out there, don't they? Those umbrellas really catch the eye. Oh, I *hope* it's going to work out!'

'Of course it is.' Mandy came over to give her arm a comforting squeeze. 'You wait, we'll be in Egon Ronay before we know it! They'll be beating a path to our door. Just keep the supplies going, that's all you have to do.'

'Yes.' Rissa turned to Donald. 'Donald, we're really grateful to you for all your help. I don't know how we'd have managed without it. Well, I suppose we'd just have done it ourselves, but it would have meant having to open a lot later and——'

'Oh, don't keep *on*,' Mandy interrupted. 'Donald *likes* doing it.' And Donald grinned at Rissa's reproving expression and said easily: 'It's all right, Rissa, I do enjoy it. Call on me any time.'

'Well, it's very nice of you. I'll remember that—while you're here. But I suppose you'll be going away soon, won't you?'

'Away?' Donald looked puzzled.

'Well, there's not much for you round here, is there? Not a lot of call for a degree in marine biology. You'll have to go away to work, as soon as you find a job.'

'Oh no,' said Donald, smiling again, 'I'm not leaving Ichrachan. I'm staying here.'

'Here?' Rissa echoed. 'But——'

'I'm going to help Dad and save up for a fishing boat. It's what I've always wanted. I've always liked the life. It'll suit me fine.'

Rissa looked at him and could find nothing to say. And the moment's awkwardness was broken by Mandy, who sat herself down at one of the tables and said gaily: 'Tea for three, please. And a selection of those famous home-made cakes and scones I've heard so much about. Isn't this a pleasant little tea-room, dear? We'll tell all our friends, won't we!'

Rissa laughed and agreed that the tea-room really

should be christened in style. And as they sat round the table, drinking tea and choosing cakes from the delectable assortment arranged on the big plate in the centre, she forgot about Donald's plans and thought only about their own.

Although even then, as so often during the past week, her thoughts were never quite free of the memory of that encounter on the shore, when she had met a force she didn't quite understand; a dark force that had called an answering response that had left her shaken and bewildered, and uncomfortably aware that there must be more to come, however much she and Calum might try to avoid it.

Donald's plans came back to her later, however, when she and Mandy were sipping a late-night drink in the kitchen which was now their living-room too—a cosy, comfortable living-room, with the Rayburn cooker letting out a gentle heat and the shabby armchairs and sofa from the parlour fitted in around it. It was lucky that Cluny Cottage had two relatively large rooms downstairs, Rissa thought, or they would never have been able to manage. Lucky too that someone had extended the tiny scullery at some time, so that her freezer could stand out there with the modern gas cooker her father had installed a few years ago. Most of Rissa's cooking could be done there, leaving the old kitchen as a more homely room.

'I must say, I'm rather shocked at what Donald told us today,' she remarked, holding her mug of hot chocolate between her palms. 'Did you know he planned to stay here?'

'Mm.' Mandy didn't look at her. 'But I don't see anything to be shocked about.'

'You don't? But he's wasting himself? Wasting all that education—a good brain. I mean, why go to university if you're going to throw it all away and become a fisherman—which is what he intends, isn't it?'

'Yes. A fisherman. A useful job, catching fish to feed

people. What's wrong with that? If he said he was going in for farming you'd have no objection.'

'That's different.' Rissa glanced at her sister. 'Mandy, you don't *approve*, do you? You don't really think he's right to do this?'

'Why not? If that's how he wants to spend his life. Look, you know as well as I do how hard it is to get jobs these days. Donald wants to work and he doesn't see why he shouldn't do something he enjoys in the place where he wants to live. He's not ambitious, in the material sense. He doesn't want to make a fortune, he just wants to make a living. And he can. So what's the problem?

'Oh, I don't know,' Rissa sighed. She finished her drink and stood up. 'It's too late for philosophical arguments, anyway. But, Mandy, I hope *you* won't be influenced by this drop-out attitude of Donald's. You know Dad always wanted you to go to university. You've got the brain and you could do well—don't let Donald persuade you that it's not worthwhile.'

'Donald wouldn't persuade me of anything,' Mandy said quietly. 'And he's not a drop-out—any more than his father is, or old Fergus. He wants to do an honest, useful job and I don't understand why you should be so much against it.'

Or even what business it is of mine, Rissa added silently as her sister passed her in the door and went up the narrow stairs. She bit her lip and took her cup out to wash. It was seldom that she and Mandy argued, seldom that their opinions differed so sharply. Or was it just herself? Ever since meeting Calum on that first evening she had been edgy, though so far she had managed to keep it to herself. But if she was going to start arguing with Mandy, making bad feeling before they had even started on their enterprise, it was a sign that she was even edgier than she had realised. She was even beginning to wonder if they had been wise after all in coming up to Ichrachan. Perhaps it would have been better to keep it as it had always been, a holiday home.

Well, it was too late for doubts now. Everything was ready for their opening the next day. And the best thing she could do was to get to bed and get a good night's sleep. She was certainly tired enough after all the hard work of the past week.

But it was a long time before she finally fell asleep, and when she did she was troubled by uncomfortable dreams in which everything seemed to be going wrong and the cottage was besieged by tourists, all clamouring for food that Rissa couldn't find anywhere; while behind them stood Calum, grim-faced, playing on some instrument she couldn't see a jangle of discordant music that drowned her frantic words as she tried to explain that they weren't open yet.

The actual opening, of course, was nothing like that and Rissa began to relax as the morning went on and a fairly steady trickle of customers began to come in. Most of them were tourists, driving up from Oban on their way through the glens, but a few local people came in too, to wish the girls well and sample the cooking. Rissa was pleased to see her scones, cakes and biscuits receiving unqualified approval, and the smell of fresh coffee wafting out of the open doors and windows seemed to bring customers in with smiles of anticipation already on their faces.

It was towards the end of the morning, during a quiet spell when Mandy had slipped out for a breath of fresh air, that Rissa heard the little bell they had fixed on the door and came out from the kitchen ready to serve the next customer. Her initial shyness was already beginning to wear off and she smiled brightly as she came through the door—but her smile faded abruptly when she saw who the visitor was.

'Good morning, Rissa,' Calum said equably.

'Calum!' Rissa said faintly. 'I—I thought you weren't going to come near us.' And, more boldly, 'Aren't you afraid of meeting a lot of tourists?'

'I thought it would be an inoculation,' he returned.

'There'll be no way of avoiding them, after all. When do the coach parties start?'

'Look, I told you, this is a tea-room, not a fairground,' Rissa snapped. 'Not that we'd object to a coach party—but as you can see, we're limited for space and it isn't likely they'll come.'

'Oh, I don't know.' He wandered to the window. 'How many can you get in here? A dozen——'

'Sixteen.'

'And about the same outside, I'd say. Yes, I think you'll get coaches before long. After all, you're only just off the main road. Couldn't be more convenient, really.'

'Calum, did you actually want anything, or is this just a social call?'

'And she's learned to be sarcastic, too,' he said admiringly. 'That's something I don't remember.'

'I never needed to be sarcastic before,' said Rissa through tight lips. What *was* it about Calum that made her behave like this, turned her into a shrew? 'But if you don't want anything, perhaps you'd excuse me, I've some scones just due to come out of the oven——'

'Then I'll have one. Hot, with plenty of butter. And a pot of coffee too, please.' He sauntered over to the display of home-made cakes and biscuits, his big body moving through the cramped space with easy grace. 'Mm, looks good. I'll try a flapjack too. I remember your mother making those.'

'Yes,' Rissa answered quietly. 'I learned a lot from her.'

'Did you?' He turned quickly and his glanced raked her. 'I wonder. Your mother was a very wise woman, Rissa. Wise and understanding. Did you learn that from her, I wonder?' His eyes glimmered under the dark brows. 'They're rare qualities in this world, I find.'

Rissa turned abruptly. 'I'll fetch your coffee.'

In the kitchen, she had to rest her hands hard on the table, leaning on them to control her trembling. How *could* he have brought her mother's memory into it like that? Didn't he know it was sure to upset her? All right, her mother had been dead now for years and Kate had done her best to fill her place—but there were still times when Rissa was overwhelmingly conscious of that aching void, and during the past few months since her father's death she had felt it all the more keenly. Didn't Calum realise that? Maybe he didn't— maybe he was just too insensitive. But she thought it more likely that he was simply being callous. For some reason that she couldn't fathom, he *wanted* to upset her, and it seemed that there was little she could do to prevent it.

Her shaking under control now, she prepared his coffee and took the scones out of the oven, noting with satisfaction that they were well risen and an appetising golden colour. She laid a tray and took it in, adding a few other biscuits to the flapjack she took from the display.

'Looks delicious,' Calum commented. 'But aren't you joining me?'

'No. I'm working, remember? I can't sit down and gossip with the customers.'

'Who was asking you to gossip?' he murmured. 'Just friendly conversation was what I had in mind. After all, we've a lot to talk about. Quite a few years to catch up on.'

'I got the impression the other night that we had nothing to talk about.'

His grey eyes moved over her lazily. 'Did you? On the premise that actions speak louder than words?'

Rissa remembered the kiss he had given her and the way she had responded, and a hot wave of shame and anger swept over her. She turned away quickly, glancing out of the window in the hope that someone might be approaching, but the road outside was deserted. Desperately trying to quell the pounding of her heart, she rapped out her words. 'That sort of action I can do well without, Calum. And I think you were right when you suggested that we should keep well away from each other. Whatever's happened to either of us in the past few years, we don't seem to get along any more. I can't imagine what brought you down here this morning.'

'Curiosity, I suppose.' His voice was still maddeningly casual, as if her words had just washed over him unnoticed. 'I wanted to see just what you'd done to the place. And I wanted to check on something else, too.'

'Something else?' Rissa stared at him. 'What do you mean?'

'Oh, let it pass.' His grey eyes moved over her again in that disconcerting, assessing manner. 'Let's just say it was an impression, that's all.' He drained his coffee and stood up, too abruptly for Rissa to move away, so that they stood disturbingly close. She felt her breathing quicken so that her breasts rose and fell; he was so close that they brushed against his chest and she backed away, alarmed by the immediate sensations that the contact produced. Calum smiled, and the smile aggravated Rissa's already stretched nerves. She twisted away, half expecting him to prevent her, but he stood still as she said shakily: 'That—that's forty pence for the coffee and thirty for the scone and flapjack. Seventy altogether.'

'And cheap at the price,' Calum counted out the money. 'Is it done to tip the proprietress?'

'Seventy will do, thank you,' Rissa said with dignity, and took the money. In other circumstances she would never have dreamed of charging Calum for a pot of coffee, but something told her that it was best to keep him at a distance, that if he came too close there would be danger. And if sparks were going to fly like this at every meeting it would be better still if he kept right away.

She turned to go back to the kitchen, and this time Calum did stop her. His hand on her arm was more gentle than it had been the other night, but she stopped at once, acutely conscious of the fire that ran through her at his touch. Her heart seemed to be pounding right into her throat and although she would have liked to tell Calum to take his hand away, no words would come.

'Rissa.' His voice was softer now, a velvet murmur. 'Rissa, there was something I wanted to say to you. The other night—I didn't actually set out with the intention of behaving like that, you know.'

'Please,' Rissa found her voice at last, 'don't think any more of it. I—I'd forgotten all about it.'

'Liar,' he said conversationally. Then, with the serious note back in his voice: 'I just wanted you to know that I don't actually go around seducing maidens in the twilight. It isn't really my style.'

'Perhaps you don't normally need to. I imagine that you get plenty of opportunities without having to resort to seduction.'

'If you like to put it that way, yes.' His voice was expressionless.

'Not that you need to resort to ordinary little tea-room waitresses, either,' Rissa went on, determined to twist the knife in her own wounds in the hope that they might be cauterised. 'I expect your opportunities are with much more glamorous ladies.'

'You could be right there.' Calum tightened his grip and turned her inexorably towards him. She looked up at him, defying him to touch her again, and saw with baffled dismay that he was actually laughing at her. His grey eyes were bright with amusement, his mobile lips twitching with the effort to repress laughter. Rissa stared at him, her resentment growing. How dared he laugh at her! She could see nothing at all funny in the situation. She brushed a hand across her face and immediately wondered if she'd left a streak of flour there. Calum gave a snort and her anger boiled over.

'All right, laugh!' she cried, pulling away from him. 'I suppose you think it's very entertaining to come here and—and tease and torment me, just when I was hoping to get my life sorted out! Well, I'm glad you find me so amusing, Calum, because from what I saw the other evening there's not much you like about life these days. Shall I tell you what I felt? I felt *sorry* for you— yes, sorry! Sorry that someone who's got just about everything still can't be satisfied and has to get his thrills from making other people miserable. But that was always your way, Calum, wasn't it? You did it to me, you did it to Alison, and God knows how many other girls you've done it to since. The great Calum Kilmartin,' she sneered, completely carried away now. 'A musical genius—but has it made you happy? I don't think so. It's just made you more and more discontented, that's what, and I thank God that I'm not like you. I'd *rather* run a tea-room and scrape a living all my life than be a genius, if you're a fair example of the breed. And I should think Alison had a lucky escape from you that summer. I——'

Her words were sharply cut off as Calum gripped her arms and dragged her close to him. The amusement had gone from his face, leaving it as hard as granite. His eyes blazed lightning as he glared down at her, and Rissa quailed, wondering what had possessed her to speak to him like that and wishing desperately that Mandy would come back.

'Leave Alison out of this,' he gritted. 'I doubt if you've even the glimmering of an idea about what went on between Alison and me, and we'll keep it that way. My God, you really are a shrew, aren't you? Did Shakespeare know someone like you, I wonder? To think I came here today to try to make things right between us——'

'Then you needn't have bothered,' she flared. 'Things will never be right between us, you might as well make up your mind to that, and I for one don't want them to be. The less I see of you, the better, Calum Kilmartin! What's gone is gone, and you can't bring it back. So let's just forget we ever knew each other as children, shall we? And keep well away from each other in the future.'

Calum's eyes searched her face and she forced herself to return his gaze, though inside she was quaking. She steeled herself to giving nothing away; he must never know how he had occupied her thoughts. Then he gave a small grunt and dropped his hands from her arms. Rissa automatically caressed them with her own hands, wondering if there would be bruises where his fingers had tightened cruelly on her bare flesh.

'All right,' he said quietly. 'You don't want my olive branch, so as you suggest we'll forget the whole thing. I won't come here again, Rissa. And if we happen to meet, I propose that we treat each other as strangers might do—politely.' He nodded and turned towards the door. 'I'll say goodbye.'

The door closed behind him and Rissa stared at the blank wooden panels. Slowly she collected up the tray and took it out into the kitchen. Her mind was numb, her senses dulled. She moved automatically, washing the crockery, drying it, putting away the coffee pot, setting the clean cup and plate back on the table for the next customers.

So that was an olive branch, she thought, staring out of the window. It hadn't been easy to recognise, but then it probably wasn't easy for Calum to extend it. What would have happened if she had accepted it? Anything? Or nothing—just that Calum might have felt more in control of his world, as he obviously liked to be.

But she wasn't part of his world—hadn't been for years. So why should he bother?

A car pulled up at the gate and a family spilled out of it, obviously on holiday. Rissa summoned up her smile and greeted them as they came in, telling them what was available for lunch and indicating a table by the window where they could see out to the loch.

Life must go on, and this was the life she had chosen. So why was she feeling so depressed?

CHAPTER THREE

By the end of the first week, Rissa and Mandy were able to look back and decide, cautiously on Rissa's part and exuberantly on Mandy's, that their business had swelled, some holidaymakers coming more than once to sample Rissa's cooking, and it seemed likely that as they became better known things would become better still.

'At least we should be able to live on it,' Rissa declared, as she finished the first week's accounts. 'After all, it's really only got to support me full-time once you get your grant. Though we might find things getting a bit thin through the winter. I wonder if there's anything else I could do then? Take in typing, or something like that, perhaps. I could always get a living-in job somewhere else, I suppose.'

'Oh, you won't have to worry,' Mandy exclaimed. 'You'll probably find local people only too pleased to buy your cakes.'

'In Scotland? Scotswomen take pride in their baking, they're not likely to want to buy stuff from a mere Englishwoman. But it's an idea, though,' Rissa continued. 'I might be able to sell to a shop in Oban. Have to give it some thought.' She leaned back in her chair and looked affectionately at her sister. 'Well, tomorrow's our day off and I suggest you take Tuesday too. Might as well treat ourselves to two days before things get really busy. What are you thinking of doing?'

'Well, as a matter of fact Donald's asked me if I'd like to go up to the islands. You know his grandparents live there. It's a bit far for a day trip—but if you really mean it about Tuesday. . . .'

'Of course I do! That's what we decided. How are you going? By car?'

Mandy shook her dark head. 'Donald's borrowing the hotel boat. We'll go up the coast—it's actually quicker that way, and cheaper without ferries. You needn't worry, Rissa, Donald knows the way blindfold, and you know how good he is in a boat.'

'Yes. I'm not worrying about that.' But there was a small frown on Rissa's smooth brow. 'Mandy——' she began, only to be interrupted by the telephone. Mandy went to answer it; from the lengthy call which then ensued, Rissa assumed that the caller was Donald.

She wasn't too sure what to make of this closeness between Donald and her sister. They had always been friends, of course, ever since the days when they had been the youngest of the small gang of children who pottered about at the loch's edge in canoes. And Donald was a likeable young man; she trusted him implicitly to see that Mandy came to no harm. But was it a good idea to let them spend so much time together? Especially with these disturbing ideas of Donald's about hiding himself away here in Ichrachan and wasting all that education. Rissa didn't want Mandy infected with such an attitude.

Well, there was little she could do about it. Mandy was eighteen and had a will of her own. The two sisters had never fallen out seriously, but the small difference the other evening had shown Rissa that where Donald was concerned she must tread carefully. Anyway, it wouldn't be too long before Mandy herself was away at university. She would get things into perspective then.

'Well, that's me settled,' announced Mandy, coming back into the kitchen. 'We're leaving first thing tomorrow morning, and I do mean first thing. I won't wake you, Rissa, I'll get everything ready this evening and creep out with the dawn.'

'Where are you staying? With Donald's grandparents?'

'Mm. I went up there once before, you remember, that summer when Alison was here. Well, I've been since, by road, but that time we went in the boat too. It was fabulous! I love being on the sea.' Mandy's face glowed with enthusiasm and Rissa stifled a sigh. She could never remember being so wholeheartedly enthusiastic about anything. Had she, as Kate had sometimes said, grown up too quickly? Had she missed something—like her youth?

'And what will you do with your day off?' Mandy enquired.

'Oh, I don't know. Get up late—potter about——'

'No cooking then,' her sister warned her. 'And no cleaning or tidying up—we did it this evening, remember? Do something different. Why not go canoeing?'

'Canoeing? But I haven't done that for years!'

'So what? It's like cycling, you don't forget it. And it's safe enough so long as you keep close to the shore and wear a lifejacket. Heavens, Rissa, you used to be our champion. Go on, be a devil! Have a little potter round. The canoes are O.K., Donald's been looking after them.' Mandy yawned suddenly and scrambled to her feet. 'Well, if I'm to get myself ready before bed I'd better get on with it—I'm nearly asleep already. Being a waitress is hard work!' She paused at the door. 'See you on Tuesday evening, Rissa. And remember—get *out* tomorrow. No working—it's a day off!'

Rissa remembered her words as she woke and stretched in the morning. Leaning up on one elbow, she gazed out of her window at the loch, lying calm as a mirror in the early light. It was low tide and wading birds picked their way daintily among the clumps of seaweed, probing the sand with delicate bills. Morning mist lay like wisps of pearly chiffon along the mountain slopes, tinged with apricot where they were caught by the rising sun. The lonely call of a curlew, planing in from the moors, sounded like a stave of music from a wooden pipe. Rissa recalled finding a curlew's nest once when she was with Calum on one of their long walks. Just four eggs, nestling in a scrape of grass, almost exactly matching their surroundings. And on another day they had almost walked over some fledglings, freckled to look like pebbles on the stony ground and fiercely protected by their suddenly aggressive parents.

She lay back. How many times had she told herself *not* to think of Calum and those happy, far-off days? Since the day he had come to the tea-room, she hadn't seen him—except as a solitary figure away in the distance. And that was the way it had to be. Donald, who seemed to know everything, had said Calum was here to work on a new piano concerto which he hoped would put his name on the map as a composer. So he probably needed to be alone anyway. And Rissa was only too pleased to co-operate!

Early as it was, Mandy had already left. Rissa considered whether to turn over and go back to sleep. But it was such a beautiful morning—and she could always have an early night tonight. She slipped out of bed, showered in the minute bathroom, and wriggled into a pair of jeans and a gingham shirt. Mandy was right—today should be a holiday. And Rissa intended to make the most of it.

The sun was higher when, after a leisurely breakfast in the garden, she wandered down to the shore. The tide was coming in now, sweeping up the loch to its head twelve miles inland. She looked thoughtfully at the water, remembering the times when she and the others would take the canoes up on the tide and picnic on an isolated beach. No roads followed the loch to its head and you could find plenty of spots where you could be completely alone to make camp. They used to take sausages and cook them on sticks over a fire, she recalled. It was a pity Morag was away and Elspeth, who worked in an estate agent's office in Oban, unavailable. As for Alistair, he was working all the hours there were as a houseman in a Glasgow hospital and rarely managed a visit to Ichrachan these days.

So why didn't she do as Mandy had suggested and go alone? The day was calm and peaceful enough and although she hadn't been in a canoe for several years it was, as Mandy had said, something you never forgot. A bubble of excitement rose in Rissa. It would be fun to paddle gently up the loch, alone with the birds and the mountains, and have her lunch on a quiet beach. Not quite as much fun as with the others, of course, but still. . . .

Making up her mind, she ran indoors to collect lifejacket and food. Everything was where it had always been kept, in the big cupboard off the kitchen, and she fished out the watertight canister too. Spare clothes? Rissa hesitated. It seemed hardly necessary. She never had capsized, and anyway, the day was going to be warm enough for it not to matter. She pushed a bikini in, then took it out again and stripped off to slip it on under her jeans and shirt. It would be nice to do a spot of sunbathing at lunchtime.

The canvas PBK canoes were in good condition, thanks to Donald no doubt, and Rissa carried one down to the shore, then went back for a paddle and her canister, packed now with food. She locked the cottage, feeling almost as if she were going on holiday. This was fun! Then she ran down to the water's edge, fitted her lifejacket and floated the canoe, settling herself on the small seat.

It was good to be on the water again, she thought, paddling gently away from the shore. You got a completely different view of the loch from what was virtually its surface. The water here was clear and shallow; she could see the sandy bed below her, with the tiny shadows of fish whipping past. The paddle dipped into the water with scarcely a splash and the sun beat down strongly on her head. Tiny puffs of white cloud flecked the blue sky. Waders, picking at the last of the sand before it was covered by the tide, rose as she approached but wheeled above her only once or twice before settling again. In a surprisingly short time she was out of sight of the cottage and moving steadily up the shore of the loch.

As she passed Kilvanie, Rissa turned her head to

watch the opposite shore. She didn't want to know whether Calum saw her or not. Her mind had been made up on that score. The teenage infatuation she had felt had completely evaporated, and even the fierce hatred that had been mostly on Alison's behalf had died away. All she felt now—she told herself firmly—was indifference. What she did had nothing to do with Calum Kilmartin, and *vice versa*.

All the same, she was glad to find herself out of sight of Kilvanie too. There was an uncomfortable feeling about passing that long white house. As if there were eyes watching her movements; a feeling she didn't at all care for.

The day passed pleasantly. Rissa knew enough of the local tides to judge when was the best time to stop for lunch and a rest before setting back on the outward tide. She chose a grassy bank and pulled her canoe out of the water, then spread a towel on the grass and slipped off her jeans and shirt to sunbathe as she ate her lunch and read the book she had brought with her. But the sun was too warm for reading; after a while she found her eyes closing, then the book slipped out of her hand and lay forgotten on the grass as Rissa slept.

She woke with a jump of alarm. The bright sun had disappeared; the sky was obscured by heavy cloud which must have gathered from the tiny puffs she had noticed earlier. The tide was running out fast and the surface of the loch, so still and calm earlier, was whipped up into a white foam by the blustery west wind which had sprung up.

Rissa stared at it in horror. It wasn't actually rough, but if she had been setting out from home she would have put her trip off until a better day. The currents on the outward tide could, she knew, be treacherous and she ought to have started back much sooner and been almost home by now. But there was no other way of getting home from here except by water, unless she chose to walk several miles across difficult country including a stiff climb across the lower slopes of the mountain. There was nothing for it but to go as soon as possible and hope for the best.

She scrambled back into her jeans and lifejacket and pulled the canoe back down to the water. It tossed alarmingly as she got into it and she almost lost her paddle. Cold with dismay, Risssa tightened her hold on it and drove the fragile craft out into the tideway.

The weather had completely changed. From a tranquil morning it had become a stormy and threatening afternoon. The sky had darkened even since she had woken, and the loch was as grey as the clouds above, the tips of the waves breaking so that the bow of the canoe plunged through them, sending water washing across the deck. Rissa wished that the PBK could be fitted with a spraydeck to keep the water out; her imagination showed her an alarming picture of the canoe filling as she struggled to paddle it through waves that grew even bigger.

At least she ought to be able to make good time, with the tide running so fast. But she soon found that it wasn't as easy as that. The wind was blowing strongly into her face, the canoe was swept out much further towards the middle of the loch than she had intended, and there the current was frighteningly swift. Rissa found that her paddling was achieving nothing more than keep the canoe stable; it was moving more and more quickly, and as the loch widened she found herself farther and farther from the shore, all her efforts to get closer to land thwarted by the waves which slopped dangerously into the canoe when she tried to turn it, rocking the boat in a manner that made it clear that capsize was imminent unless she kept facing seaward.

There seemed to be nothing she could do but simply sit there and allow herself to be swept out to sea. Rissa glanced around desperately, but there was no one in sight and she knew from experience that distances were so great in these parts that she was probably nothing more than an insignificant speck on the water to anyone standing on the shore.

She wondered if it might be possible to make for the opposite shore. There was no road there, but at least it would be dry land and she could walk to safety. The current certainly seemed to be swinging her in that direction. With fresh heart, she paddled hard, keeping the canoe easing gradually away from Ichrachan. It would be a near thing, if she did make it; the wind was blowing harder than ever and the waves were now terrifyingly big, slapping hard against the frail hull.

She was making slow but definite progress when she heard the snarl of an engine somewhere behind her. A boat! With a gasp of relief, she twisted quickly in the seat to see whether the boatman had actually noticed her—and the canoe wobbled, lurched and turned right over.

The water was achingly cold and Rissa knew a surge of blind panic as she felt herself dragged over, head down, the canoe above her with her legs and feet still in position under the canvas deck. She had to fight to keep her head, holding her breath as she gripped the sides of the craft that had suddenly become a trap, drawing her feet free and twisting her body clear. But she mustn't let go of the canoe—to lose it in these waters would leave her perilously alone—and as the lifejacket's buoyancy brought her to the surface she clung to the wood and canvas, aware that her breath was now dangerously short and that if she didn't get air soon she would be unable to help choking on the water that roared in her ears.

But the roaring as she scrabbled her way out of the canoe could have been either the water that surged around her or the boat's engine as it came alarmingly close; Rissa had no way of knowing. She clung to the tossing craft, pulling herself up it and gasping as her head came clear of the water, blinking and pushing the hair back from her face. The ducking had been so sudden and unexpected that she felt she'd swallowed half the loch, and she was too concerned with choking out the water and getting her breath back to wonder at first about the boat. When she did begin to think again, it was in panic in case the boatman, whoever he was, *hadn't* seen her—in which case her position was very serious indeed, for it was unlikely that she could survive long in these waters unless she could get the canoe right way up again and get back into it, and she knew that such an operation wasn't easy even in calm waters.

As these thoughts raced through her mind, Rissa's vision cleared and she turned her head anxiously—and breathed a great sigh of relief. The boatman had seen her and was almost level with the canoe. The two craft tossed together as he leant over and grasped her firmly by her shoulders, dragging her without ceremony over the thwarts and dropping her like a sack of not very precious goods in the bottom of the boat.

At that moment, it didn't even matter that it was Calum Kilmartin who had come to her rescue. It didn't matter, either, that his face was dark with fury. All Rissa could think of as he hauled her roughly into the boat and dumped her on the bottom boards was that she was safe. And that Calum—Calum, whom she had loved and hated, and never really been indifferent to, no matter how she had tried—had rescued her.

'Oh, Calum,' she gasped, feeling like a landed fish. 'Thank God—I was getting really scared, I——'

'Stop jabbering and keep still,' he ordered sharply. 'I don't know if you realise it, but there's one father and mother of a storm blowing up and it's *not* the weather I'd choose for an afternoon out. So just be quiet while I get us ashore.'

Rissa subsided meekly. She really didn't feel like arguing now—and she knew that Calum was right. The heavy clouds were scudding rapidly across the sky now and the boat rocked violently on the increasingly rough sea. It wasn't a large boat and the engine was labouring hard as they forged through the waves. But it felt a good deal steadier and safer than the flimsy canoe, and Rissa lay there, shivering but thankful, and confident that Calum would soon have them back ashore.

With the help of the engine it didn't take long, and she was soon gratefully aware of the scrape of shingle under the keel. Calum turned off the engine and jumped into the water, dragging the boat swiftly up the beach, getting it well above the tideline and fastening the painter to a large rock. Only when all was secure did he turn his attention to Rissa.

'All right,' he said curtly. 'You can get out now.'

He didn't extend a hand to help her, and she scrambled over the side of the boat and dropped to the beach. Her wet clothes clung to her uncomfortably and she couldn't wait to get out of them and into something dry. She pushed back clinging hair and turned her head, wondering if Calum had brought her back to Cluny Cottage or to Kilvanie.

But to her astonishment, she was at neither of these places. And as she looked around she realised that there was no sign of habitation along the shore. It was wild and lonely, the slope of the mountain coming right down to the loch, and there was no road, nor even a track.

She turned and stared at Calum, her heart pounding in sudden fear.

'Where are we? I don't recognise this at all.'

'I don't suppose you've ever been here before.' His tone was peremptory. 'We're on the opposite side of the loch from Ichrachan, and rather further down towards the ferry at the mouth.'

'The *opposite side*? But why? How are we going to get home?

'We're going to wait till this storm blows itself out.' Calum looked up at the sky, almost black now. 'And before that we'd better find ourselves some shelter. We're both pretty wet and it won't be funny sitting out here while that lot empties itself all over us.' He grabbed her arm, none too gently. 'Don't stand there snivelling, Rissa. There's an old shepherd's hut somewhere along here, if I'm not mistaken, we ought to be able to find some shelter there.'

'I'm *not* snivelling——' she began indignantly, but Calum was taking no notice. He tossed her a large tarpaulin sheet and, heaving a large plastic box into his arms, set off along the beach. Rissa had no choice but to follow him. Half sobbing with cold, reaction and frustrated annoyance, she stumbled after him, feeling very chilled now, her legs stiff and weak. The thought of spending hours alone on this deserted shore with Calum frightened her, and she would have given anything to be back in bed with the day still ahead of her. But miracles like that didn't happen, and somehow she was going to have to get through the rest of this nightmarish experience with nothing and nobody to help her.

Calum led her, at a fast pace which made no allowances, along the shore until he reached a small stream which tumbled down from the mountain slope above. With a small grunt of satisfaction, he turned to follow it up a shallow valley and a few minutes later, to her relief, Rissa caught sight of the old shepherd's hut.

The rain was driving down now, blotting out most of the view, and she was glad to reach the thick stone walls. But her relief turned to dismay when she realised that the hut was partly ruined and that the only shelter it offered was in one corner, with barely room for two people.

'This'll do,' Calum declared, ignoring her gasp of dismay. 'It'll have to, there's nothing else.' He began to unpack the plastic box. 'Good thing I keep a survival pack in the boat. It won't be luxury, but it'll keep the rain off us at least.'

Numb with horror, Rissa did as she was told. The tarpaulin, when fixed with heavy stones, formed a kind of tent—but it was very small, and the thought of sharing it with Calum made her tremble. She looked at him with mute appeal, and an expression of exasperation crossed the craggy features.

'*Now* what?' he demanded, and Rissa shook her head. 'Nothing, I just—oh, why did we have to come *here*?'

she burst out. 'Why couldn't you have taken me home? It'll be hours before we can get away now!' The wind whipped her wet hair round her face as she spoke and a low rumble of thunder muttered behind the mountain.

'*That's* why,' Calum hit out at her. 'For God's sake, girl, haven't you *any* sense? You go off in a canoe, *on your own*, with no message left so that anyone knows where you might be——'

'There was no one to leave a message with, Mandy's away!'

'—and then you totally ignore all the warning signs, leave it far too late to come back——'

'I fell asleep!'

'—and get caught first in a tidal race that you must have known would occur with a westerly wind against an outgoing tide, and then in a storm that you'd have known was brewing if you'd only taken the elementary precaution of listening to the weather forecast before you set out. Just what were you playing at, Rissa? You're not a tourist—you know these waters and how treacherous they can be. Have you completely lost any sense you might ever have had, or were you trying to prove something? You could have been killed—as it is, you've lost a perfectly good canoe.'

'No! It was nothing like that—I just forgot. It was such a lovely morning, I'd no idea there'd be a storm, and I still don't see why you couldn't have taken me home——'

'I *told* you! Because I *did* know there was going to be a storm and I knew that the chances were we'd never make it. And it seemed a good chance to make *you* realise one or two things, too!' His face was blazing with anger and Rissa felt her own temper rise to match his as she faced him in the wind and the rain.

'And just what are those?' she demanded. 'Just what do you think I ought to realise, Calum Kilmartin?'

'You ought to realise that the sun doesn't rise and set on whatever *you* happen to be doing, that's what! And you ought to realise this——' He took a step towards her and before Rissa could guess at his intention, he had her in arms that were like bands of steel around her body. She struggled ineffectually, but before she could protest his lips were on hers, hard and demanding, showing no mercy, his mouth forcing hers open with sheer insistence. A fury such as Rissa had never before experienced took possession of her body and she twisted violently in his arms, all too aware of the arousal of his body as he pressed against her. Then a white-hot flash of lightning split the sky above them, followed immediately by a crack of thunder that drove them apart, and Rissa dived under the tarpaulin for cover.

Calum was beside her before she could do more than collapse in a frightened heap in the corner, and his big body seemed to fill the tiny space. His hands were on her at once and she struggled and pushed at him, but he gave an exclamation of annoyance and said impatiently: 'All right, Rissa, calm down. Obviously that wasn't the right moment—but I'm not trying to rape you. I just think you ought to get out of those wet clothes. I don't want you catching pneumonia. Look, I've got a space blanket here——' He took a small package from the box and began to unfold it. 'Get those wet things off and wrap this round you.'

'Wh-what about you?' Rissa was shuddering with cold, her teeth chattering and she knew he was right, although the thought of being here in this confined space, naked, with Calum, was more terrifying than anything that had happened yet. 'You're just as wet.'

'I'm aware of that. I'm also aware of the fact that you'd die rather than let me share the blanket.'

Rissa hesitated. She wanted to tell him he was right—but she couldn't bring herself to do that. And although Calum wasn't *quite* so wet as she was, his jeans were clinging to his legs where he had jumped into the water, and the rest of him was damp from the rain that had begun to fall. 'You—you can share it if you like,' she said at last, meekly.

Calum's teeth flashed in the semi-darkness. 'Don't worry, Rissa. I'm tough, I'll survive. Now——' he rummaged again in the box '—let's see what else I can produce. A thermos of hot soup—another of coffee—and some emergency rations in the shape of nuts, dried fruit and chocolate. Sorry I couldn't manage any more, but as you see space was limited.'

Rissa stared at him. 'A thermos of coffee and soup?' It sounded delicious, but just at present she wasn't concerned with that. 'You mean you *expected* this to happen?'

'It never does any harm to look ahead,' Calum said calmly. 'Rissa, are you going to get those wet clothes off or shall I do it for you?'

She squirmed away from him, pressing her back against the cold stones, but the look in his eye told her he meant business and, reluctantly, she began to undo the buttons of her shirt.

'You might at least turn your head away,' she muttered, feeling scarlet colour warm her cheeks as she caught his eyes on her.

Calum grinned. 'Do you think I've never seen the naked female form before?'

'No, I certainly don't! But you haven't seen mine, have you?'

'Oh, I doubt if it's so very different from the rest,' he drawled maddeningly, but as Rissa bit her lip in frustration he did turn his head and close his eyes while she wriggled out of the wet shirt and jeans. Her bikini was soaked too, and with a wary eye on him she pulled that off too and quickly wrapped herself in the space blanket which, although almost as thin as silk to enable it to be folded into a small space, immediately warmed her with its high insulation. She hugged it round her, her shivering already lessening, and Calum opened his eyes again.

'And now perhaps you'll answer my question,' she said coldly. '*Did* you expect to be marooned here with me? Because if so——'

'I could have engineered the whole thing,' he finished mockingly. 'But of course I did, dear Rissa, I called up the weatherman as soon as I saw you paddling upstream this morning, looking like a mermaid of the loch, and arranged for a storm to catch you on the way down. What else did you imagine——'

'Oh, don't be ridiculous! You know what I meant.'

'Yes, I do, and the answer's yes and no. Yes, I did half expect that you'd get caught and need rescuing, so I made what preparations I thought necessary and kept an eye on the loch for your return. When you didn't appear and the storm was obviously approaching, I thought I'd better come out and look for you. You took some finding in those waves, too, I may say. No, I didn't anticipate being marooned. If I had, I'd have brought more than just emergency rations, I can assure you. But since it has happened then I suggest we both make the best of it and act like civilised beings.'

'Like you did just now!' Rissa flashed, and he inclined his head.

'Yes, that may have been mistimed. But I still maintain that you ought to acknowledge what's happened between us. In my experience, there's usually only one way to resolve such a situation.'

'What situation?' Rissa stared at him, baffled, but at the same time she was aware that her heart had begun to thump alarmingly. Calum looked at her; his grey eyes were intent and involuntarily she pulled the blanket closer around her.

'Don't pretend you don't know,' he murmured. 'It's only chemistry, I know—but you can't deny it's there. This powerful physical attraction between us. It's tormenting you as much as it is me, isn't it? Keeping you awake at nights; gnawing away at you when you'd rather be thinking of other things. Oh, it's all happened before, I know—but there's only one way to get a fever like this out of the system. And that is. . . .' He let his voice trail away but there was no mistaking his meaning and Rissa shivered again, though this time not with cold.

'I don't know what you're saying,' she managed, and he laughed shortly.

'Don't you? Then you must be very innocent indeed, dear Rissa, and for a girl of twenty-three in this day and age I find that unlikely. You know full well what I mean. Let the fever rage, that's the only way; let it run its course and enjoy what it brings. And then, when it's burnt itself out—well, we each go our own way, none the worse for the experience. Don't you agree?'

Rissa gasped. As a proposition, it was just about the most coldblooded she'd ever come across—not that she'd had many anyway. Was this how Calum behaved with those other girls, the glamorous society women he was so often photographed with? Was that the way *they* behaved? If it was, she was heartily glad she'd never moved in such circles, nor was ever likely to.

'Well?' Calum repeated. 'Do you agree or don't you?'

'I most certainly don't! I never heard of anything so outrageous—and in any case, none of it's true. Not as far as I'm concerned, anyway. I'm sorry if it's the way you feel, Calum, but there's really nothing I can do about it.'

They stared at each other. Outside, the storm still raged around the mountain, lightning filling the makeshift tent with flashes of aching white, the thunder drowning their words with an explosion of energy, so that they had to shout at each other to make themselves heard. Rissa saw Calum's lips move but heard nothing except the roar outside; as it died away he repeated what he'd said.

'You're wrong, Rissa. Whether you're aware of it or not, you're wrong. You feel it too—don't you think I can tell by the way you react to me, the way you respond when I kiss you? Do you really believe that such a feeling could be only one-way? And you know as well as I do that there's only one way to deal with it. So why not make the most of it?'

'Keep your distance, Calum Kilmartin,' Rissa

muttered between her teeth, but his hand was stroking its way down her arm and she had to close her eyes to prevent him seeing the pleasure it gave her. Painfully, she turned her head away, and Calum's hand came up to cup her cheek and turn it back. His face was oddly gentle as he moved closer to her and she was acutely aware of her nakedness. The feel of his fingers on her bare skin sent a delicious tremor through her body; she lifted her face, wanting to beg him to stop, to leave her alone, but no words came; instead, as her lips parted he brushed his own against them in a gesture of tenderness that took her completely by surprise. The tremor deepened and she gave a little sigh as his lips moved against hers. What was the use of resisting it, after all? Calum could overpower her in seconds if he wished; there was nobody for miles and the storm was raging just as fiercely outside, the rain beating a rapid tattoo on the stretched tarpaulin sheet. And did she even want to resist it—really? Her senses wheeled giddily as Calum's kiss became more and more intimate, his hands moving sensuously over her soft skin, and with a little moan she let her own arms slip around him, not caring that with the movement the blanket slipped down between them, leaving her rounded breasts exposed to his gaze. For a brief moment he stared downwards, then he bent his head and laid his mouth between the quivering curves, and Rissa felt a shudder pulse through her entire body. She arched towards him, pulling him closer, exulting now in the feel of his lips and hands going where they would, and when he drew back to unbutton his damp shirt she helped him with eager fingers, gazing with delight at his broad, deeply-tanned chest, letting her hands move in random exploration through the curling dark hairs, wanting only to feel its hardness against her again.

'You do agree, don't you, sweet Rissa,' Calum breathed in her ear as he stretched himself beside her again. 'This is the only cure—the only way to find peace—you know it as well as I do. . . .'

And as his words penetrated her consciousness, it was as if a cold clear light illuminated Rissa's mind. She saw plainly what she was about to do—give herself to a man who didn't love her, and never even made pretence of it; who simply wanted to use her body to rid himself of a torment, as he might take a medicine to cure an irritating rash. And he had swept her along with him! She, who had always vowed that the man she slept with would be the man she married. No chance of that with Calum, she knew. So why was she letting him seduce her—and not simply letting him, *encouraging* him!

Calum's hands were inducing the most exciting sensations she had ever known, and it wasn't easy to resist them—but with a quick movement she twisted away from him, cramming herself close into the corner, the hard stones of the wall pressing uncomfortably into her back as she stared at him through the brilliant flashes of lightning. She saw the surprise on his face fade, to be replaced by a dawning anger, and she spoke quickly, determined that this time *she* would be the one to do the talking.

'Oh no, you don't!' she gasped through clenched teeth. 'All right, I admit it's there—this physical attraction you talk about. But I can tell you this, I don't want it—and I'm not going to cure it your way, not if I have to spend the whole night out on the mountainside! I've never slept with a man yet, Calum Kilmartin, and I shan't till I find someone I can really love—and someone who loves me. And you most certainly aren't that man! So just find someone else to cure your frustration, because I'm not that desperate. And if *you* are—well, maybe *you'd* better spend the night on the mountain, then you'll have something else to think about!'

She dragged the blanket round herself again and met his eyes defiantly. Another shaft of lightning speared the darkness and the thunder cracked, so close that it sounded as if the mountain itself were collapsing around them. Rissa gave a cry of fear, staring at the flimsy roof with wide eyes. At that moment she longed more than ever before to be in Calum's arms, held close and safe from the violence of the elements. But she could not let herself move back to him; there was another kind of violence in the tent even more terrifying than that without. Despairing and helpless, she buried her face in her hands and waited.

When Calum touched her again it was with a gentleness that took her once again off guard, and if he had persisted she might then have given way to him. But he didn't. He merely drew the blanket closer around her, tucking her in as if she were a child, and his voice was quiet as he spoke.

'All right, Rissa, don't be frightened. We're safe enough here. And I won't worry you any more.' He paused, and then asked in an unusually hesitant voice: 'Was that true, what you said? That you've never slept with any man?'

'Yes,' Rissa replied, her voice muffled. 'Yes, it is true. I suppose you think I'm very old-fashioned, but I can't help that. I've just never wanted to.' *Until now*, she should have added, but knew that there was no need. The words hung in the air between them.

'A lot of good things are old-fashioned,' Calum said reflectively, almost as if speaking to himself. 'But we won't discuss it any more. I think we'd better try to get some rest, don't you? And a hot drink wouldn't do us any harm. What do you fancy—coffee or soup?'

They sat together in a kind of truce, drinking the scalding soup from plastic mugs that warmed their hands. The steam warmed the tent too, making a fug that was cosy in contrast with the fury outside, and Rissa found her thoughts drifting inevitably back over the day's events. She had experienced real terror when she had been alone in the canoe, tossing on the broken waves and unable to reach the shore, and she realised now how lucky she had been that Calum had watched for her. Nobody else had known of the danger she was in; if he hadn't come to her rescue she would probably have been drowned by now, swept out to sea, her body perhaps never to be seen again, to be washed up in some lonely cove where it might or might not be found.

'Calum,' she said, turning impulsively towards him, 'I never thanked you for saving me. I—I do realise what a fool I was. If it hadn't been for you——' Her voice broke and he slipped a comforting arm around her shoulder, patting her reassuringly.

'All right, Rissa. It's over now—nearly, anyway. This storm will blow itself out overnight and we'll be able to get back in the morning. By the way, where's Mandy? The cottage was locked up when I went to see if she knew where you were going. Did you say she was away?'

'Yes—she's gone up to Donald's grandparents for the night. Oh—I wonder if they got there before the storm? If anything's happened to Mandy——'

'It won't have. Not if she's with Donald. I take it they left in good time? You were out pretty early yourself.'

'Yes—I should think they got there before the weather changed.' Rissa relaxed, hardly noticing that she was leaning against Calum's shoulder, her soft flesh touching his. Warmth emanated from his body, and the soup had given her a glow within.

She felt suddenly, overwhelmingly tired, wanting only to give in and sleep. And after all, why not? She'd had a long and exhausting day; fear and emotion had drained her strength. And, strangely, she knew that Calum no longer presented a threat—for the time anyway. Why not sleep? Her eyes closed; she was dimly aware of Calum drawing her closer, as she turned her cheek slightly into the hollow of his shoulder, breathing in the sharp, male scent of him, and slept.

It was light in the stone and canvas shelter when Rissa finally awoke, and she lay still for several minutes, wondering vaguely where she was. A dim recollection of a rough sea, a violent storm and an emotional upheaval that almost transcended the thunder and lightning formed a confused jumble of impressions in her mind. Not that any of it really mattered; she was snug and comfortable where she was, her body enclosed by something that held her firmly yet lightly, a protection against danger; her skin warmed by something that pressed lightly against her from shoulder to toe, something that had an exciting roughness about it yet felt as if it belonged there at her side, something animal that gave comfort and yet promised far more; something. . . .

With a quiver of panic, Rissa realised that it was Calum who lay so close to her. One arm was under her head, holding her cheek pillowed on his shoulder; they were each half turned, curling into each other's body, so that Rissa was lying in his lap, his other arm across her waist with his palm resting lightly against her stomach. And it didn't take her more than a second to realise that he was as naked as she was.

Rissa lay perfectly still, afraid to move, afraid to wake him. She remembered everything now—the rescue, the way Calum had brought her here to this lonely spot (and she still wasn't convinced that that had been necessary), the storm and his attempt at seducing her. A chemical thing, he had called it; a fever, for which there was only one cure. And she had almost given way: a deep shame washed over her as she recalled her own behaviour and admitted that Calum might have good reason to suppose that she agreed with his diagnosis and prescription.

And then, somehow, there had been a truce. She had eaten chocolate, drunk soup and felt better. She'd apologised for the trouble she'd caused, thanked him for rescuing her. And then—she didn't remember anything else, but she must have fallen asleep and Calum had taken his own jeans off (well, they *were* wet, she remembered wryly) and got under the space blanket with her.

So now what? Did she wake him and demand to be

taken back at once? The storm had obviously subsided; it was quiet outside and a weak sunlight filtered through the tarpaulin sheet. Or did she just stay still and wait for him to wake first, and hope that he didn't attempt again to take advantage of the situation?

Rissa moved slightly against him and felt again the delightful warmth of the contact of skin against skin. If only things could be different, she thought hazily. If only Calum had said he loved her, what a difference it would have made. She'd sworn that the man who possessed her would be the man who loved her—oh, if only it could have been Calum. . . .

And then the full meaning of her thoughts hit her like the thunderclaps that had raged around the mountain last night. The man who loved her, she'd said—and the man she loved. And she knew then with a blinding clarity that her near-surrender last night hadn't, after all, been purely physical. Because Calum *was* the man she loved. He had been her hero as a child; she had been infatuated with him as a teenager; she loved him now as a woman. And that was why she responded to him so ardently, why his touch was like fire on her skin, his kisses like wine on her tongue.

She loved Calum Kilmartin with a deep, abiding and enduring love. And she closed her eyes as the pain began, creeping over her with an agony that she knew would be with her always. Because it was a hopeless love too. Calum had never mentioned the word. It didn't seem to figure in his life at all; the bitterness she had seen in him at that first meeting would prevent him ever acknowledging it even if he did feel it.

For her and Calum there was no hope, no hope at all. And Rissa wished heartily and sincerely that she had never returned to Ichrachan and Cluny Cottage; had never, never met him again.

CHAPTER FOUR

As Rissa lay there, still enclosed in Calum's sleeping embrace, it dawned on her that they would never again lie together like this. Oh, if Calum had his way they would—perhaps many times. But it wouldn't be for ever. And she knew that once she had allowed Calum to make love to her, she would be wholly and totally committed; and although her heart was already telling her that there could never be another man for her, she couldn't let it happen. Not if she were to go on living any kind of life.

She stirred restlessly, and then immediately froze as her senses told her that Calum was waking. A wave of dismay swept her body as he murmured something in her ear and tightened his hand on her stomach. The fingers moved gently, exploring as if he too were puzzled to wake up like this; then a tiny grunt escaped his lips and she felt his mouth against her ear.

'Mm . . . what a way to wake up! It *is* Rissa, isn't it?'

The voice was still sleepy but already held that cool, mocking note that maddened her. Before he could tighten his hold further, Rissa had wriggled free and was out of the blanket, shivering as the cool morning air struck her bare skin. She glanced wildly at Calum and caught his eyes on her in a frank and appreciative appraisal that had a blush travelling over her whole body as she turned to scrabble for her clothes. They were still soaking wet, of course; she couldn't face the jeans, but she dragged on the damp bikini, wishing that Calum wouldn't watch her with that bright, amused glance.

'Better now?' he enquired when she had the bikini in place, and she glowered at him.

'I'll be better still when I can get back to the cottage.

69

I take it we *can* go back this morning—the storm's died down completely.'

'Certainly we can go back.' His voice was lazy and he made no attempt to move. 'I'm only sorry you can't canoe, but it would have been impossible to tow in the conditions we had yesterday.'

She didn't even bother to answer that. She would have liked to rip the blanket off him and force him to get up, but memory told her all too clearly that he was naked and she didn't quite have the courage. Tossing her head, she said with as much dignity as she could muster, 'I'll just go outside. It won't take you long to get ready, will it?'

'No, not long. You go and have a look round, but don't get chilly. Might be an idea to hang your shirt up out there for a few minutes; you'll need some kind of covering in the boat.' He sat up and stretched himself and Rissa's eyes went to the firmly-muscled torso, the powerful arms. 'Go on, then,' he added, glinting a look at her. 'Unless you want to come and give me a good-morning kiss. . . .'

Rissa fled. Behind her, she could hear Calum's deep chuckle, but she didn't wait for more. She pulled on her sandals and wandered down to the shore to see that the boat was still safe. It would be disaster if anything had happened to that!

Thankfully, she saw that it was still there and the tide, though now running out again, wasn't too low for them to make the journey across the loch to Ichrachan. In the clear morning light she could see now where she was; rather nearer the loch mouth, as Calum had said, and on a shore which she had never before visited. During their childhood excursions they had never ventured this far down, knowing that the currents could be treacherous. In any case, it wasn't the most alluring of places, with the grey rocks of the mountain sloping right down to the shore and stretches of scree making exploration almost impossible.

Rissa turned and went back to the little valley, where

Calum was now once more clad in jeans and busy folding up the space blanket and tarpaulin. He nodded briefly to Rissa as she came up to him and handed her the second thermos.

'Pour out some coffee, will you? That's a pretty good flask, it should still have some heat in it. Afraid that's all there is till we get back.'

'Perhaps I ought to cook you a breakfast as a thank-offering,' Rissa said tentatively, not sure whether she wanted him to accept or not.

'Perhaps you should at that.' His eyes rested on her thoughtfully. 'Don't seem to have got much else out of our little jaunt, do I?'

'Only the thought that you probably saved my life,' she retorted. 'Or maybe that doesn't matter so much? I seemed to be rather a thorn in your flesh, after all.'

'I have an idea that you'd rather it had been almost anyone else who'd saved you,' he drawled. 'But it wasn't, and since we both seem to want to get away from each other as soon as possible I suggest we make tracks. Would you mind carrying the flasks? These things won't fold as small as they did before and there's no room in the box. Oh, and I hung your shirt up, though I don't suppose it's dried much.'

Exasperation tingled through Rissa as she collected the shirt and pulled it round her shoulders. Why couldn't he have left it? Why did he always have to be in the *right*?

She followed him back to the boat and they made the crossing in silence. It was another beautiful morning, the waters of the loch calm and clear again after their turbulence. The beaches were tinged with pink from the glow of the sunrise, and Ichrachan, its roofs touched with the same pearly blush, looked like an illustration from a fairy-tale. Rissa looked up the loch towards the mountains which loomed like great guardians around the long inlet they protected, and a lump rose in her throat. How beautiful it was, she thought; and how romantic! If only she and Calum could be returning in different circumstances, with different feelings about each other; after a different kind of night together.

Well, they could have been. But she knew that to give herself to Calum without having his love would be a betrayal of herself, and her feelings for him. It was something that couldn't—mustn't—ever happen.

'I won't come in for breakfast,' Calum observed as he nosed the boat up the shingle, close enough to be able to jump ashore. 'I think it's better that way, don't you?'

'Yes,' said Rissa, her voice small. She wanted to touch him, to make him look at her, to get back to some kind of relationship with him—but it was no use. He kept his face firmly averted, once she was safely ashore he turned back to the boat.

'Be seeing you,' he said casually, and Rissa nodded, her heart too full to speak. She watched him walk away down the shore; tall, broad and bronzed. And it was as if he was walking out of her life.

Slowly, she turned back to Cluny Cottage, unlocked the door and went inside. It seemed longer than twenty-four hours since she had set off up the loch in the old canoe, and she sighed a little to think that she must now get things ready to open the tea-room in a couple of hours' time—and without Mandy's help. But it was just as well she'd suggested her sister have the second day off, since it had meant she was away for the night and therefore knew nothing of Rissa's adventure.

Rissa went upstairs to her bedroom. She would have like nothing better than to slip into bed—her night at the lochside had left her stiff and sore—but instead she showered and washed her hair, feeling a good deal better when she had done so, and dressed in a fresh blouse and skirt of pale cream with a lime green flower pattern sprinkled over it. It brought out the golden lights in her hair and she smiled ruefully as she looked into the mirror. Who would imagine now that she had spent the day before getting half drowned and the night under a tarpaulin sheet at the foot of a mountain!

By now, she was hungry. She went down to the

kitchen and heated a couple of rolls from the freezer, making coffee at the same time. A quick check told her that there were enough scones and cakes to see her through the day, since with Mandy absent she wouldn't have time to cook. Soup for lunches was already thawing—Rissa had begun by making huge batches and freezing them—and there was plenty of cheese and pâté. She took some more rolls out and put them in a large box, then sat down to eat her breakfast.

A knock sounded at the door just as she began, and she felt herself turn cold. Surely it couldn't be Calum? But before she could move, the back door was opening and a face peered round it; a pale, slightly freckled face with a tuft of floppy brown hair above it.

'Hi, Rissa,' the newcomer said. 'You needn't look so transfixed, you know. I'm not a ghost.'

'Alistair!' Rissa leapt up and dragged him into the room, her hands on his shoulders, then gave him a hug. 'But what are you doing here? I thought you were in Glasgow, being a doctor, and never got any time off?'

'True, true and nearly true,' he answered, grinning. 'But they do occasionally let me out for a breath of fresh air, and when I heard that you and Mandy were back—well, I just had to come, didn't I? Are those rolls your own baking? They look delicious.'

'And I suppose you're hungry, as usual.' Rissa handed him the plate and fetched another for herself. 'It *is* good to see you, Alistair. When did you arrive? You haven't driven up from Glasgow this morning, have you?'

'Er—no.' To her surprise he looked uncomfortable. 'As a matter of fact, I arrived yesterday. I did call round in the evening——' he glanced at his plate '—but you were out. Or perhaps you were away? Donald's mother told me he and Mandy had gone up to the islands and she thought perhaps you'd gone too.'

'No, I didn't.' Rissa found his discomfort infectious. Rapidly she debated whether to tell him what had happened, but it was all so complicated and so stupid, and anyway she wanted to forget it. 'I spent the night with a friend,' she said at last, but to her surprise this seemed to embarrass Alistair even more. She wondered why: she did have friends in the area, after all. But there was no way now of altering her statement and she changed the subject by asking about his work. 'It's such a long time since I've seen you. There must be heaps to catch up on.'

The odd moment passed and they were soon chatting away in the old manner, laughing and teasing each other as if they'd been apart for weeks rather than years. Oh yes, it was right to come back to Ichrachan, Rissa thought as she poured him more coffee and listened to his hilarious account of life as a houseman in a large hospital. This was her place. And Calum wouldn't be here for long; without his presence haunting her, she would soon settle down.

'Well, it's lovely to have you here, but I'll really have to get on with my work,' she said at last, getting up to wash the breakfast things. 'Come back tonight and have a meal with us, Alistair. Mandy'll be back then and I expect she'll ask Donald to stay. Do you know, those two decorated the tea-room all on their own in just a week? They've made it lovely, too.'

'I've got a better idea,' Alistair declared, following her to admire the décor. 'I'll give you a hand until Mandy comes back. Yes, I will,' he added as she began to protest. 'I've nothing else to do and I worked at just about everything while I was at medical school. Waiting, washing-up, general dogsbodying—you name it and I've done it. Where shall I start?'

'Well, if you really mean it you can make salad,' Rissa suggested. 'There's a great pile of lettuces outside and all the other things in the fridge. Put it all in separate bowls—here—and then I can just make them up as they're ordered. Thanks, Alistair. That'll be a great help.'

It wasn't long before the first customers began to arrive, and Rissa found herself too busy for gossip. She flitted in and out of the tea-room, serving coffee, scones and cakes, while Alistair washed a mound of lettuce, sliced tomatoes and cucumber, and cut cheese into large chunks. Rissa and Mandy had decided to serve only simple lunches to begin with, until they could see just what they were able to cope with, and so far their platters of salad, cheese and pâté with home-made rolls and toast had proved a great success. After all, as Mandy observed, most people on holiday ate large breakfasts and went back in the evening to substantial Scottish dinners, so a light lunch was really what they wanted. Not that it was all that light by the time they'd sampled one of Rissa's delicious desserts, she had added with a mischievous grin, but the girls had to live!

Alistair stayed at the cottage for the rest of the day, sampling almost everything Rissa produced, and when she finally closed the door behind the last customer just before six o'clock he insisted on helping with the washing-up. They finished the task in companionable silence. It was pleasant having Alistair around, Rissa thought. He was the kind of nice, easy-going man who would make someone a good husband one day.

It wasn't long before Mandy and Donald arrived, full of their two days away, and Mandy greeted Alistair with delight. Unfortunately, Donald couldn't stay: he had promised to help his father that evening. The three of them worked together to produce a meal, with much laughter and noise; and it was because of this, perhaps, that nobody heard Calum arrive after supper until he opened the door and stood there surveying them.

Mandy was the first to notice him. She was on her knees in front of the Rayburn, surrounded by a pile of photographs she'd dragged out from somewhere—photos of them all as children, growing up together. 'Look,' she was saying, 'don't you remember that day, when we caught that huge sea-trout? There's a picture of Rissa holding it up. We cooked it on the beach and it was delicious.'

'Mm, it was.' Alistair took the album. 'But who took the photo?'

'Why, Calum, of course! He was there too, don't you remember?' Mandy turned her head quickly, her dark hair belling against her cheek, as the kitchen door swung open. '*Calum!* Well, talk of the devil!'

'I take it that's a compliment.' Calum came into the kitchen, his eyes on the little group by the stove, and Rissa got up quickly. He was so tall, she felt at a distinct disadvantage when he towered over her like that. 'What's the cause of my name coming up?' He hadn't looked at Rissa and she busied herself in pouring him a mug of coffee.

'We're looking at old photos. Remember this one? And this?' Mandy passed the book up to him and he studied the picture expressionlessly. Then he handed it back.

'I remember—the days of innocence. Thank you.' He took the coffee and sat down in an armchair. Rissa hesitated, then dropped back to the rug beside Alistair. She was in her own home, for goodness' sake! Why should Calum Kilmartin influence her choice of seat? But there was no doubt that his arrival was affecting her strongly; her heart was thumping like a carpenter's hammer and her palms felt clammy. Why had he come? Why couldn't he leave her alone to get over her feelings in her own way?

'On leave, Alistair?' he enquired pleasantly, and Alistair nodded.

'For a couple of weeks, barring national disasters or an outbreak of the plague.' To Rissa's surprise he wasn't speaking as easily as he had been with her and Mandy; in fact there was a return to the uncomfortable manner he'd shown with her for a few moments, earlier. But before she could think about it, Calum had gone on smoothly.

'You'll be wanting to get some fresh air and exercise, then. Pity I can't join you, but I'm busy just now working on some music—a piano concerto which I hope will be performed at the Edinburgh Festival.'

'Is that right? I'd like to hear that,' Alistair said

eagerly. 'In fact, I walked up to see you yesterday evening, but you were out. . . .' His voice trailed off and he looked embarrassed again. Calum glanced thoughtfully at him, then at Rissa, and smiled slightly.

'Yes,' he said, 'I was out. I spent the night with a friend.'

Rissa almost groaned aloud. It had to be coincidence that Calum had used exactly her own words, but there was no way she could tell Alistair that. And now she understood the cause of Alistair's embarrassment—he'd been to both Cluny and Kilvanie, found them both out and assumed they were together. Why he should do that, she didn't know—unless he remembered that old childhood passion she had had for Calum—but again there was no way of telling him the truth. She bit her lip. Alistair was so nice. She'd rather anything than have him think—well, whatever it was he did think.

But again, she was given little time to worry about it. Mandy had brought the talk back to past days and Rissa was forced to join in. Then they passed on to what they'd all been doing since, and hoped to do in the future. And it was at that point that Mandy dropped her bombshell.

'No, I've decided I'm not going to university,' she said in answer to Alistair's question. 'And if you don't mind I'd rather not say any more just at present—my plans aren't all that firm at the moment.'

Rissa was jerked out of her introspection. 'Not going to university?' she echoed. 'This is the first I've heard of it. Of course you're going, Mandy, it's all arranged.'

'Not completely. I haven't had my A-level results yet, so——'

'But you'll have done well, and you've had offers from several universities. You'd made up your mind which one to take——'

'And now I've made up your my not to take it.' Mandy's blue eyes looked at her. 'Rissa, I'm sorry to spring this on you, I didn't mean to say anything until it was all decided——'

'You mean you weren't going to give me a chance to object!'

'No! Well—I suppose partly. Oh lord, I wish Donald had stayed after all. It would've been so much easier——'

'Donald? Then he's involved in this? Mandy, I warned you——'

'Please, Rissa, don't let's say any more about it now.' Mandy's small face was determined, and Rissa sighed. When that mulish look settled on her younger sister's features it was a sure sign that there were battles ahead.

'Look, it's time I went,' Alistair said diplomatically. 'Shall I come in again tomorrow, Rissa, or will I be in the way?'

'You could never be in the way, Alistair,' Rissa said warmly, her mind still on Mandy's revelation. 'But you don't want to spend your holiday slaving away here.'

'Don't I?' he said innocently. 'I thought I did. Makes a nice change from bodies. See you tomorrow, then. Nice to see you, Calum.' He nodded and let himself out.

'I'll be going too,' Calum announced, coming to his feet in one swift, lithe movement. 'Rissa, I'd like a word with you, please.'

'Must it be now, Calum?' Rissa was reluctant to go outside with him, as he so plainly intended; she wanted to stay and find out just what was in Mandy's mind, and she didn't want to be alone with Calum anyway. Why should she—what could they possibly have to say to one another?

'Yes, now,' he said inexorably, and in case of any argument took her wrist and drew her towards the door. There was nothing she could do—she didn't want a scene in front of Mandy.

'I won't be long,' she said, but Mandy was already tidying the room.

'I'll go on up to bed. Please, Rissa—I don't want to talk about it tonight.' And Rissa, feeling that there was nobody who would help her in this crisis, had to allow herself to be taken outside like a child going reluctantly home from a party, confusion, dismay and humiliation combining in her to tie a hard knot of anger somewhere in the region of her stomach. And it was only natural that the recipient of her anger should be the man who was exerting this force on her.

'Would you mind letting me go?' she hissed as soon as they were out of earshot. Along the lane, she could see Alistair walking home, and prayed that he wouldn't turn round. 'Just let go of my wrist! There are enough wrong impressions going round about us as it is!'

'Are there?' Calum's voice was amused. 'How's that?'

'Oh, you must know! Didn't you see Alistair's face when you said you'd spent the night with a friend? It was exactly what I said when he told me he'd been here. Now he's convinced we spent the night together——'

'But we did!'

'Oh, you *know* what I mean!' she cried. 'Heaven only knows what he thinks we were doing——'

'I should imagine you have a very good idea what he thinks, or you wouldn't be getting so uptight. I can't answer for Heaven, of course——'

'Oh, stop *laughing* at me! It isn't funny—it's—it's——'

'Well, what is it?' he probed when she floundered into silence. 'Tragic? Catastrophic? Hardly, dear Rissa. So Alistair's got the wrong idea about us. As a matter of fact, I'm glad to hear it—because I've been wondering about you and him.'

'Alistair and me? What on earth are you talking about?'

'I don't see that it's such an outlandish idea. He's been with you in the cottage all day, hasn't he? Alone?'

'Along with a steady stream of customers, yes. Dreadful, isn't it!'

'You didn't have customers all the time. I expect there were a few quiet patches.'

'During which we did erotic and immoral things like wash dirty dishes, make more salad and fill little pots with jam,' Rissa supplied sarcastically. 'You're not going to tell me you've got photographs of these disgusting activities, are you? Perhaps you mean to blackmail me.'

'Sarcasm doesn't suit you, Rissa,' Calum observed. He took her arm and wound it round his waist, turning in its circle so that they stood close together, and despite herself Rissa felt her pulses race. 'Did you know that Alistair was coming up this week?'

'No, I didn't. How should I? I haven't kept in touch with the people here—we just come together when we're all here, it's always been like that.'

'Except that you haven't been here for several years. Yet you and Alistair spend a whole day together and look like childhood sweethearts at the end of it, curled up on the rug together. Are you sure you haven't been in touch meanwhile, Rissa?'

'Yes, I am, and I don't see what business it is of yours anyway!' Rissa tried to pull away, knowing that it would be useless. She'd matched her strength against Calum's before and found it hopeless. 'Look, what is it to you what I do? Who I meet and keep in touch with? We're nothing to each other, you and I——' And that wasn't true, only he mustn't know. She turned her head aside as Calum's face loomed nearer, and added bitterly: 'I *wish* you'd leave me alone. I'm not your property.'

'No,' Calum murmured, and now he was disturbingly close, 'but you will be, one day.'

A kick of fear jolted through Rissa's body. 'What do you mean by that?'

'Just what I say. Look, we've had all this out before. This—this feeling there is between us—there's only one way of resolving it. I've told you that. It's the best thing for both of us, Rissa. Once it's burned out, we can live our own lives again. Leave it to fester and it could be disaster.'

'For you, perhaps,' Rissa rapped. 'Not for me. For me, it would be disaster to give in to your peculiar arguments.' She stopped abruptly, mentally kicking herself for having said too much. Calum mustn't know how she felt—if he once suspected she loved him, that his merest touch turned her bones to water, there would be no defence against him. All the advantages were on his side, but fortunately he didn't know it—must never know it. As long as he kept on thinking that it was plain physical attraction—*lust*—on her side too, there was a chance of safety. . . .

'Would it indeed?' Calum said reflectively, and she quivered, dreading his coming to the correct conclusion. 'And just why would it be disaster for you to have an affair with me, Rissa? Tell me—I'm interested.'

Well, there was only one answer to that. 'Because as lovers go you'd be a long way down my list of top twenty,' she flashed. 'In fact, I doubt if you'd make it to the bottom. Oh, I may not have gone the whole way with anyone yet—but that doesn't mean I've no experience at all. And so far nothing you've done or said has given me any hint that you could even begin to turn me on! So an affair with you—even one night— could be nothing else *but* disaster, for me.'

Calum's eyes narrowed dangerously as she spoke. 'Stop talking nonsense, Rissa,' he ordered harshly. 'You've responded to me like a fire lighting. Do you really think I can't tell? I'm not without experience myself, you know. I know just what a woman——'

'The sort of woman you normally go around with, perhaps. But I'm different, Calum. All right, I've led you on a bit—but that's all. It didn't mean a thing. If you thought it did—well, I'm sorry. But I don't suppose it'll do you any harm at all to be deprived of what you want, just once in a while. And this is the once.'

They stared at each other, Rissa's topaz eyes meeting the steel-grey of his probing glance with a bold defiance she didn't really feel. All those lies she'd told! Could he really be deceived? Could he really believe she'd been acting—leading him on? It was something she knew she would never do—but as long as Calum believed her capable of it, that didn't matter.

'You scheming little bitch!' he snarled at last, and a

fresh wave of fear shook her slim body. Had she gone too far, angered him too much? 'So that's your little game. Lead 'em on, and leave 'em. And how many other poor unfortunates have you tried this on, Rissa? Just what kind of twisted pleasure does it give you anyway?'

'You'd be surprised,' she answered cheekily, then gasped as he grabbed both her shoulders and shook her violently. 'Calum, don't! You're hurting me!'

'And I'd like to hurt you a damn sight more than that,' he rasped. 'Such a sweet, innocent little face, too. Such a pure little body. My God, Rissa, you've got a lesson coming to you—and I'm damned if I'm not the one to teach it!'

'Calum, no!' Rissa cast an agonised glance up the shore, where the lights of Cluny Cottage showed that Mandy was now in her bedroom. The curtains were drawn while she got ready for bed, but Rissa knew that soon her sister would be drawing them back so that she could lie and gaze out at the loch. She couldn't bear that Mandy should witness this scene down on the beach. Calum followed her glance and grunted; he let his hands fall from her shoulders, and Rissa hastily took a step back. She watched him warily, but he made no attempt to detain her, standing there with his hands in the pockets of his corduroy trousers and glowering from under hooded brows. His expression was unreadable.

'All right, Rissa,' he said at last. 'You go in and take it out on that kid sister of yours. Harangue her for wasting her opportunities, or whatever it is you're going to say. Just remember, while you're doing it, that it's your own frustration you're talking about and not her future at all. Because that's the price of the little game you're playing, Rissa—frustration and bitterness. You'll achieve nothing else by playing with men as if they were fish and never making the final landing.'

'And what about you? Aren't you playing with women? Using their bodies for your own satisfaction, taking your pleasure and then discarding them like broken toys?'

'The women I *use*, as you call it, are mature women, not sentimental children. They know just what they're doing and they *use* me just as much as I use them—if use is the right word at all, which I doubt. They understand something you don't seem to, Rissa—that the human body is furnished with certain biological functions and needs which it can be very pleasant to gratify, and which if ungratified can turn very sour indeed. I think my way will prove to be best in the long run—both for myself and the women who share my gratification.'

'And doesn't love come into it at all?' Despite herself, Rissa couldn't prevent a note of longing entering her tones.

'To some extent, yes. I wouldn't have an affair with a woman I wasn't fond of in some way. Affection, liking, I'd say, rather than love. I haven't actually experienced that rare commodity yet.'

Lucky you, Rissa thought, but she merely said aloud: 'And when you do?'

'That,' Calum said distantly, 'will be a different situation, and will be entirely my own business.' His needle-bright eyes glinted at her under the heavy brows. 'Well, is the interrogation over? May I go now?'

'I never asked you to stay,' she flashed, and to her fury saw him grin. Oh, if only he wouldn't keep *laughing* at her! She'd rather make him angry than that, but she'd done her best and seemed to have only just ruffled his maddening composure. Wearily, she turned away.

'Rissa.' His voice was soft and she turned back, unable to suppress a quick leap of the heart. 'Don't be too hard on Mandy,' he went on, and her spirits sank again. That softness hadn't been meant for her after all, and she'd been a fool to imagine it ever would be. 'She's young, but she knows her own mind and I suspect she knows how to make a success of life too.'

'And I don't? You don't understand, Calum. I've been more or less responsible for Mandy for years, ever since our mother died. Oh, Dad did his best and Kate was marvellous—but I'm Mandy's *sister*. I've had to think for her, and this—coming on top of everything else——' Her voice broke suddenly and she put her hands up to her face. She was aware of Calum's footsteps crunching on the shingle, felt his hands on her shoulders, but couldn't move. Didn't even know why she should. The big hands grasped her shoulders lightly, the thumbs moving with curious gentleness over her collarbones, and she wanted to rest her head on the broad chest and weep. But it was out of the question; and after a moment she drew a shuddering sigh, lifted her face and moved away again.

'Goodnight, Calum,' she said, and this time he made no attempt to detain her.

'Goodnight, Rissa,' she heard as she moved away up the beach. She didn't look back until she reached the door of the cottage; and when she did, the shore was empty, as if no one had ever been there.

Rissa didn't see Calum again for several days. She went through her work like an automaton, getting up each morning to begin the cooking and preparation for the day's customers, helping Mandy with the waiting, washing up in the extension to the kitchen. It was almost as if she were two people: the normal, everyday Rissa who smiled, chatted, joked and even laughed, and the real, private Rissa who kept her feelings to herself and, deep inside, ached for a love she could never know.

Alistair came in as he'd promised to and proved a tower of strength, although after the first two days Rissa put her foot down and banned him from coming in the afternoons. 'You need some fresh air and exercise,' she told him. 'This is your *holiday*, Alistair. I can't have you going back to Glasgow more overworked than when you left.'

'Oh, rubbish, I'm fine,' he said, but Rissa shook her head firmly.

'You're not. Would you tell one of your patients to work full-time in a busy tea-room as his holiday? Of course you wouldn't. And you owe it to your patients to look after yourself—you won't be much good to them otherwise.'

'It's not me you're thinking of at all, then,' Alistair said sorrowfully, and Rissa smiled.

'No, not you at all,' she agreed. 'So that's settled, then. You can come in the mornings, but after that you've got to go away. And it won't be any use coming back and ordering afternoon tea, because we won't serve you!'

'All right, I'll do as I'm told. On one condition.'

Rissa eyed him warily. 'And that is?'

'That you come out with me on Monday. Mandy says you close then and have a day off. I thought we'd walk up the valley and have a nice lazy day by the river.'

'Well, we were thinking of staying open on Monday,' Rissa hedged. 'It seems silly to close when there are so many people about.'

'All the same, you'll be having a day off,' he persisted. 'Mandy's told me she and Donald will cope. You see, you've really no choice, Rissa, we've got it all planned, so you might as well give in.'

'So I see. All right, then.' It would be nice to have a day out with Alistair, she admitted to herself. During the past week or so they'd grown very close and she felt at ease in his company. None of the tensions that troubled her when she was with Calum; none of the prickling excitement, the heightened awareness, the unfamiliar emotions. Yes, Alistair was good for her.

All the same, she sighed a little when she thought of Calum. If only it were possible for them to enjoy a day together without those tensions, that conflict that lay so close to the surface, ready to be sparked off like a dangerous firework. It had been like that once. Why couldn't it be again?

No doubt Calum would say that it was because they had both grown up, because they were aware of each other as man and woman, because the chemistry between them was too strong to be withstood. Well, probably he was right. But was he also right about the solution?

Rissa let her mind play with the idea of letting Calum make love to her as he so obviously wanted. She had experienced enough in his arms to know that it could be a true fulfilment for her, that Calum roused her as no other man ever had—maybe ever would. Shouldn't she listen to her body's demands, go along with what both she and Calum yearned for and risk the consequences?

To do that, she would have to go to Calum and tell him how she felt. She would more or less have to ask for his favours. A surge of heat coloured her cheeks at the thought. It would be just like Calum—this new, bitter Calum—to reject her then, just for the pleasure of seeing her humiliation. No! That was something she couldn't face. She would just have to live without the experience of lying in Calum's arms, totally united. Not that there could ever be total unity between two people who quarrelled all the time, she reminded herself quickly. Nor between two people who didn't love each other equally. Love on one side—hers—wasn't enough. And the damage could be irreparable.

Also on Rissa's mind was the problem of Mandy. Somehow there still hadn't been time for that discussion Rissa meant to have. Mornings were a rush to have breakfast and do a few chores before opening the tea-room at ten-thirty—earlier if, as had happened once or twice, people were already arriving with hungry looks on their faces. After that, they were busy most of the time, for quite a lot of people called in at the little harbour town of Ichrachan on their way up from Oban to the Highlands; and with no other place to get refreshment for a long way, barring the hotel which attracted a different kind of customer, Cluny Cottage was ideally situated. There was no time to talk seriously during the day. And in the evenings, both were too tired to do more than have their own meal and relax for a while before falling into bed.

Nevertheless, they would have to talk. And as Mandy seemed to have arranged neatly for Rissa to be out on the whole of Monday, when she had hoped for a short time off, at least, it looked as if the issue would have to be forced into the open.

Consequently, she made it clear to Alistair that he would be more welcome in his own home that evening. They would be fairly safe from Donald, who was working in the hotel during the evenings, and Rissa determined that this time Mandy would not be allowed to escape.

But in spite of her determination, Rissa found Mandy just as stubborn as she'd feared, and the discussion left her feeling dissatisfied and angry.

'I know just what you're doing,' Mandy observed as soon as they had cleared away the supper dishes and were sitting in their armchairs with mugs of coffee. 'You want to start getting at me about university. Well, you can save yourself the trouble. I've made up my mind.'

'But, Mandy——' Rissa felt helpless at her sister's unusually belligerent tone '—you can't just decide something like that without consulting anyone.'

'I can. I'm eighteen.' The small, vivid face looked set and obstinate, and Rissa sighed.

'It's not just that, Mandy. This has been planned for years. You've worked for it. You know how pleased Dad was when you did so well at school, how he'd looked forward to you going to university. You've always been the one with the brains——'

'So why aren't you letting me use them?' Mandy's tone was abrupt and Rissa stared at her. 'I mean it, Rissa. You say I've got brains, yet you won't let me think and decide for myself how I want to live my own life.'

'But you're so young,' Rissa objected. 'And you're throwing away an opportunity hundreds of girls would give their ears for——'

'That's not a fair argument. It's like making a child eat too much dinner because a lot of little boys in India are starving. It's an impertinence. Besides, my giving up—I won't say throwing away—that opportunity makes it available for one of those others, doesn't it?'

'Yes, but—oh, you're getting me all confused!' Rissa put her hand to her head.

'That's because I'm the one with the brains,' Mandy said smugly, then looked contrite. 'I'm sorry, Rissa, I didn't mean it like that. But I really have given this a lot of thought, you know. It's not just a sudden whim. I'm just not at all sure that having brains means a university education is desirable. It might not always be a good thing—for every kind of brain, or for every kind of person. I don't think *I'm* the kind of person it would be good for. And I think I know myself pretty well.' She glanced up and her bright blue eyes met Rissa's. I didn't do so badly when I suggested we come up here, did I? Doesn't that prove something?'

'So far as I can see, it just means that you're in love with Ichrachan,' Rissa said slowly. 'And that's just the danger. There's nothing here for you, Mandy. It's fine for me—I'm doing what I was trained for and it gives us both a home we love. But you—you could do so much more.'

'You're wrong,' Mandy said quietly. 'Ichrachan has everything I want, and all I want to do is here.'

'I suppose you mean Donald. He's at the back of all this, isn't he—him and his drop-out ideas!'

'And there's no need to speak like that, Rissa! Yes, Donald *is* involved—but why shouldn't he be? You know we've always been friends—well, you haven't been here much in the past few years, so perhaps you don't. But Donald and I have always known we'd marry some day. I've always known that where he went I'd go too—it's just marvellous that he's chosen to stay here, where I want to be more than anywhere else. And I won't need a university degree to be his wife, so why should I go away for three whole years when it's *now* he needs me?'

'Marry? You and Donald? But you're——'

'Too young,' Mandy finished bitterly. 'Don't bother to say it, Rissa. Well, according to the law I'm not. Donald and I could marry tomorrow if we wanted to. But we'd really rather you were happy about it too,' she added coaxingly. 'Honestly, Rissa, you've nothing against him really, have you?'

'No—I like Donald, of course I do. He—he'll make a good husband, I've no doubt.' Rissa felt bewildered; she was losing control of the situation and she didn't like it. Mandy had always been her responsibility; Rissa had looked after her ever since they were quite small. She could even remember Mandy as a baby, could recall giving her a bottle. Now Mandy had taken the reins out of her hands and Rissa felt rather as if she were behind a runaway horse, with no idea at all as to how to bring it under control.

'Dad wanted you to go——' she began feebly, repeating what she'd said earlier, but this time Mandy interrupted her.

'Look, Rissa, don't let's get sentimental over this. Yes, I know Dad wanted me to go to university, but if he'd been alive now I'd have felt just the same and we'd probably be having the same argument! I'm sorry if this upsets you—I don't like saying it myself—but just because he's dead it doesn't mean I can't live my own life the way I want to. I don't have to condemn myself to three years that will be wasted—yes, *wasted* as far as I'm concerned, just because Dad would have wanted me to. How do you *know* he'd have wanted me to, anyway? Don't you think that he, of all people, would have encouraged me to make up my own mind, without interference from other people?'

She panted into silence and the two sisters gazed at

each other. Then Mandy lifted her hands in a curious, helpless motion. 'I'm going to bed now,' she muttered. 'But think about it, Rissa—just think about it. Because you're going to have to accept it, you know. Nothing will change my mind.'

CHAPTER FIVE

It was a relief to close the door of Cluny Cottage behind her on the following Monday and get into Alistair's car for her day off. The weather had turned misty and cool, the mountain tops shrouded in heavy cloud, and it wasn't a day for walking. Instead, Alistair told her, they would go for a drive and have lunch out somewhere.

'It's time you sat back and let someone else cook you a meal and wash up after it,' he declared as they drove away. 'And Mandy and Donald will cope perfectly well at Cluny. A very capable young pair, that.'

'Mm.' Rissa couldn't help the doubt creeping into her voice, although she knew that as far as the cottage was concerned Alistair was right. He glanced at her sharply.

'Still worrying about Mandy?'

'Well, of course I am! She's talking about throwing up everything, Alistair, and she's so young. She hasn't even *tried* being independent, and she wants to tie herself down here——'

'Just as you have,' he suggested mildly, and Rissa sighed with exasperation.

'That's just what *she* says. But what's right for me isn't necessarily right for her, is it? Alistair, I feel so helpless. She's made up her mind and it seems that nothing I can do will have any effect.'

'So don't do anything.' Alistair drove up the twisting road between the shadowy mountains. 'Let Mandy make her own decision. Wouldn't you have wanted to do that, when you were eighteen?'

'Yes, but I never wanted to drop everything and get married——'

'But if you had,' Alistair persisted. 'We can't help when we fall in love, you know.'

Rissa opened her mouth to speak, then caught his eye. There was something in his expression that made her hesitate. Suppose Calum had wanted her five years ago—wanted her to marry him, follow him all over the world, make his life hers. Wouldn't she have done so?

'I still think Mandy ought to go on with her plans for university,' she insisted. 'It's quite different. She's not being asked to leave the country or even to leave Ichrachan. She could still come back and marry Donald in three years' time if they feel the same then.' She bit her lip, wondering if she'd given herself away then, but Alistair said nothing for a few minutes. He slowed down to let some hill sheep cross the road, then spoke again, his voice quiet.

'It isn't just that, though, is it, Rissa? There's more than Mandy worrying you. Like to tell me about it?'

'I don't——' Rissa began, then stopped. It wasn't fair to lie to Alistair; he'd been kind to her, a real friend. He deserved the truth.

'Yes,' she admitted. 'There is something else—but I don't think talking will do any good. It's something I have to work out for myself.'

Alistair pulled the car off the road and on to the short, tufted grass. He stopped the engine, then turned and looked at her, his face grave.

'You can tell me to mind my own business if you like,' he said, 'but I think I can guess what it is. It's Calum, isn't it?'

Rissa nodded, her eyes suddenly full of tears.

'I don't know what's been going on between you, but it strikes me you're getting hurt,' Alistair went on. 'You're beginning to look strained and unhappy. Isn't there anything I can do?'

'No,' she whispered. 'I've just got to get over it on my own.'

Alistair sighed. 'But that's just what you don't have to do. Don't try to carry these burdens all alone, Rissa. Let someone share them.' His voice deepened and he moved a little closer and put his fingers under her chin, lifting her face towards his. 'Let me share them.' And his lips touched hers; softly at first, then with increasing pressure.

Rissa sat quite still, bemused and astonished. She'd never dreamed Alistair could be feeling like this! She'd looked on him as a close friend, nothing more. How could she have been so blind?

Alistair lifted his lips from hers and looked down into her eyes. 'I don't know just what was between you and Calum,' he murmured, 'but if it's over now, why not let me heal the wound? I've always had a feeling for you, Rissa, and this past week I've realised just what that feeling could be. Don't you think you could love me, Rissa? Just a little? Enough—perhaps—to marry me?'

'*Marry* you? Rissa stared at him, too astounded to say more, and Alistair grinned ruefully.

'I see that the notion hasn't even entered your head. But now that I've put it there—well, do you think you could at least consider it? Oh, I didn't mean to say all this just now—but you looked so sad. And I'm sure we could be happy together. Look at the way we've been this past week—and I've always believed that if a couple can get along in the kitchen they can get along anywhere!'

Rissa couldn't repress a smile at that. 'You're probably right,' she agreed. 'But—marriage—Alistair, I just don't know. . . .'

'Well, at least it's not an outright refusal. And I do mean it, Rissa. I'd do everything in my power to make you happy. You will think about it, won't you?'

'I—yes, I suppose so, but I——' Any further words were lost as Alistair caught her to him and kissed her again. Rissa slipped her arms round his neck; the least she could do was find out if he could stir her senses, if she could envisage loving him in the way that he wanted.

Alistair's lips moved against hers and Rissa stroked the back of his head. But there was nothing; no white-hot fire, no tingling, no surge of desire. And as she moved away her attention was caught by another sound; the sound of an engine as a car headed towards them along the narrow road.

'Ignore it,' Alistair muttered, drawing her close again. 'Rissa, my sweet——'

But Rissa's eyes were open as he kissed her again. And she felt a barb of dismay as the car came round a bend and drew level with them. It wasn't going fast and she recognised it instantly—and groaned inwardly as for a brief instant she met the driver's eyes.

Calum Kilmartin's BMW cruised by like a shadow on the road. Calum Kilmartin's grey eyes, razor-sharp, looked at and took in everything as he passed. And from the expression on his face, Rissa knew that he was far from pleased.

Alistair didn't press the subject after that. He sensed Rissa's lukewarm response to his kisses and let her go, saying that he wouldn't rush her, there was all the time in the world for her to make up her mind. And he was probably right too, she thought as he started the engine again. There would never be any settling of the conflict that was between her and Calum, and he certainly wasn't about to make any proposals. Propositions were more in his line, and he'd made that. The ball was now in her court—and that was where it was going to stay.

Alistair took her around the head of the loch and on to Inveraray, where they had lunch at a hotel, overlooking the water. Afterwards they wandered round the little town, exploring its craft shops and climbing to the top of the church tower. They had tea in a small tea-room in which Rissa's professional interest amused Alistair enormously, then they took a leisurely route home, stopping on the way for dinner and arriving just as dusk began to fall.

'Thank you, Alistair. That was a lovely day,' Rissa said sincerely. 'It's done me a lot of good to get away for a few hours. I love Cluny, but one does need a change now and then.'

'Good.' He put his hand on her shoulder and watched her intently. 'And—you will think about it, won't you? I know I'm not in the same class as Calum—but I would make you happy, Rissa, if it lay in my power at all. And I'm sure it does.'

'Yes.' Rissa glanced down at her hands. 'I will think about it, Alistair. And—thank you for asking me.'

He leaned forward and gave her a light kiss. 'Goodnight then, Rissa.'

'Goodnight, Alistair.' She got out of the car and waved as he drove away; then she turned to go into the cottage.

'A very pretty little scene! Quite heart-touching!'

Rissa stifled a scream and leapt back as she recognised Calum. He had been standing in the shadow of a rowan tree and now moved forward into the light. There was a sneer distorting his handsome face and he held himself tautly, as if suppressing some fierce emotion.

'Calum! What are you doing, skulking there?'

'Waiting for you, of course. I'm surprised you didn't ask the boy-friend in. After all, he practically lives here, doesn't he?'

'That's none of your business!' she blazed.

'I think it is. Or if not, I'll make it so. It was a pretty little scene I saw this morning too, as I drove up the glen. Or were you too busy to notice me?'

'I saw you,' Rissa said shortly. 'And I'd be glad if you'd stop spying on me, Calum. As I said, it's none of your business. Now, please let me pass.'

'Not until we've had a little talk.' He glanced around. 'Unless you think this isn't the place for such a discussion as we're going to have. . . .'

'I certainly do, but as I don't intend to have any discussion at all with you that hardly matters—let me *go*, Calum! What on earth do you think you're doing? Let go of my wrist!' She struggled angrily, but the iron fingers clamped all the tighter and she was half dragged along the lane to where Calum's car stood, just out of sight of the cottage. 'I'm not coming anywhere with you, Calum, so let go of my——'

'Get in,' he said curtly, and opening the door he shoved her through like a sack of potatoes. Rissa collapsed on the seat in an ungainly heap, then struggled to regain her balance and get out again, but before she could open the door he was in the driving seat and had started the engine. The car moved forward and she swung round furiously.

'Where do you think you're taking me? Do you realise this is out-and-out kidnapping? Let me get out— I'm not coming anywhere with you—stop the car at once!'

'I'll stop when I'm good and ready,' he told her imperturbably. 'So you might as well stop that yelling, Rissa, because no one's going to hear you. You needn't worry, I'm not taking you up to my mountain lair. Only to Kilvanie.'

'Kilvanie?' Rissa hadn't been to Kilvanie more than three or four times in her life. Old Mr Kilmartin had never encouraged visitors, and even when she had gone there, usually with some kind of message, she had never penetrated further than either the kitchen or the hall. 'What are you taking me to Kilvanie for?'

'I told you, to talk. It's the only place I can be sure we won't be interrupted.' Calum drove swiftly through the darkening lanes and turned off up the little track that led only to Kilvanie. 'And don't try to run when we get there, Rissa. I'd only have to run to catch you and it would be too boring. You won't get away, you know.'

Rissa said nothing. She had in fact been planning to do just that, and once again he had frustrated her plans. But she'd get away somehow, she vowed. Nobody was going to hold her prisoner, least of all Calum Kilmartin.

The car swept into the drive and she looked at the long, low house, white in the gloaming. It wasn't a house that should be lived in alone, she thought irrelevantly. It was a family house, a house that ought to have children running in and out, laughter floating through its windows. For a brief moment she played with the idea of living here herself, her family around her—children with black hair and grey eyes. . . . She snapped her thoughts away from such dangerous channels. It wouldn't happen. Couldn't—because Calum's thoughts were as different as it was possible to be.

She followed Calum into the house. It was pleasant inside; he must have cleared out a lot of old Mr Kilmartin's heavy Victorian furniture and replaced it with simple, good pieces that went with the style of the building. Colourful rugs lay on the polished floors and a few interesting pictures hung on the walls. But Rissa didn't have time to examine them as Calum led her into a comfortably furnished living-room with french windows that looked out to the loch. Perhaps it was through these that he had seen her heading up the loch in her canoe a week ago.

This was obviously the room that Calum worked in; a grand piano stood near the window, with score sheets scattered over it. Many of them bore scribbled notes of music, and Rissa moved nearer and stared at them in fascination. The notes looked like a flight of swallows, perched on telegraph wires as they made up their minds to set off on their long journey to Africa; some of them seemed already to have taken flight, the others were impossibly crowded together. The wild jumble seemed to indicate—hazily, she recalled school music lessons— a highly complicated piece of music and, though it might sound discordant to her ears, she was forced reluctantly to concede that it must require considerable skill to play.

Calum was standing by the door, watching her. He hadn't put a light on and his face was a pale blur in the dimness. There was something calming and restful about the room, something that surprised Rissa who hadn't expected to find anything calm and restful around Calum. Was there another side to him, a side she hadn't suspected—or had once known and then forgotten? She remembered the times when he had touched her with unexpected gentleness, the times when she'd felt that it needed only the right word from her to break through that barrier to the real Calum underneath.

Hesitantly, she took a step towards him; then stopped, dismayed, as he spoke and she realised that his voice was as harsh as ever.

'Well, Rissa? Maybe now you'll tell me just what you're playing at. With me—and with young Alistair.'

'Alistair?' She was bewildered, then angry. 'That's none of your business!' she flashed. 'And I'm not playing at anything.'

'No? Rissa, just what kind of a fool do you take me for? Twice I've seen you today, and each time you've been—well, to put it nicely, canoodling with Alistair. Dear knows what you've been doing the rest of the time——'

'Perhaps you should have followed us more assiduously,' Rissa cut in sarcastically. 'You might have learned something!'

'Yes, I just might—I might have learned that you're an out-and-out bitch, ready to take it from any man!' Calum stepped forward suddenly and had her by the arms before she could move. 'Any man except me,' he said silkily. 'Or shall we change that situation right now?'

'No, we will not!' Furiously, Rissa writhed in his arms, but she knew that there was no way she could free herself from that iron grip. 'Calum, if you brought me here just to—to——'

'As a matter of fact, I didn't.' He sounded suddenly tired, and loosened his grip. 'I brought you here to talk—but somehow that doesn't seem possible between us, does it?'

'So perhaps you could take me home again?' Rissa suggested sweetly. She stood where she was, held loosely in the circle of Calum's arms, and didn't try to escape. When he held her like this, she didn't want to. It felt so right, so natural, and she didn't want to move. But she knew it couldn't last.

'No, I must get this sorted out, for my own peace of mind. Rissa, what is it with you and Alistair? He's at Cluny every day, you spend your day off with him, I see you in his arms not once but twice—and you say you're not playing with him. So what the hell is it, do you mind telling me?'

His voice grew tense again as he spoke the last words and Rissa felt a shaft of pleasure that she had apparently succeeded in upsetting that maddening equilibrium. Serve him right! It might show him that he wasn't, as Alison had once called him, God's gift to womankind. It might do that oversized ego of his a lot of good.

'Yes, as a matter of fact I do mind telling you,' she answered coolly. 'It's a private matter between Alistair and me. But as I can see that you're prepared to use brute force to find out, I suppose I'll have to. Alistair asked me to marry him today. *That's* why I say I'm not playing with him.'

'To *marry* him?' Calum's eyes darkened. 'And have you given him an answer?'

'No, not yet. I said I would think about it.'

'I see.' His voice was grim. 'You'll think about it. You'll keep him on a string, playing him along, taking whatever he likes to give you, and you'll *think* about it. And then, when he goes back to Glasgow, still without his answer, you'll write him a nice, friendly letter. *Sorry, Alistair, but I've thought it over and I have to say no. I find we're not really suited, but I shall always look on you as a brother.* And you say you're not playing with him! It's just as I thought, Rissa—you're nothing but a grubby little scalp-hunter!'

'I'm *not!*' His hands had tightened on her arms again and she wished she'd escaped while she had the chance. Defiantly, she stared up at him, though already there was a niggling little feeling of unease in her mind. Was he right? Was that what she would have done? 'But it wouldn't have been like that,' she cried, as much to herself as to Calum. 'I *was* going to think about it—I didn't want to hurt him.'

'Then you shouldn't have strung him along——'

'I didn't!'

'So why did he ask you to marry him?' Calum demanded savagely. 'He must have had *some* reason for thinking he had a chance.'

Rissa turned her head away, drooping suddenly. 'I don't know. I never realised he felt that way, I swear it. I—I just didn't think of it.'

'No. And that's your trouble, Rissa. You don't think. Or rather, you spend so much time thinking about the things that worry *you* that you haven't any thought to spare for other people.' Calum released her abruptly and ran his fingers through his black hair. 'My God, Rissa, don't you have any idea at all what you can do to men? Do you still not have any idea what you do to me?'

Rissa stood still, watching as he went to the piano and riffled through the sheets of music scattered over it. He sat down and struck a powerful chord that vibrated through the room, through her body and into her very soul. '*This* is what you do. I've been trying for weeks now to work out a particular theme—a theme that's been on my mind for a long time. At last I was really getting somewhere—and then you came along, and *this* is what happens!'

His hands covered the keys and the violent music shattered the silence. The chords thundered across the room, filling it with a sound so primitive and elemental that Rissa felt her whole body shake. Blindly, she found a chair and sank into it, her mind numbed by the insistent repetition of a theme that was already beginning to speak to her, though she could not understand its message. It ran like a thread through the thunder, catching at her heart with a loneliness that brought a lump to her throat, then rising on a crescendo of hope but never quite reaching a climax; never quite finishing, but returning to that isolated theme that brought an ache to her throat before thundering out again with such savage violence that she gasped as if in pain.

The music left her weak, but just when she felt she could stand no more it changed once again and she heard a passage sweet and tender enough to bring tears of a different kind. This was music she could understand, she thought, lying back in the chair with eyes closed; it was beautiful, unlike anything she had ever heard before, and it was trying to tell her something—but again what the message was she could not grasp. And then there was another change, a change that flung her cruelly back into the despair that had been only hinted at in the first passage but was now there in full force, so that she felt as if she had been cast into a deep, black pit from which there would never be any escape; and as the music crashed to an end she found herself crouching in the chair as if threatened, her hands clenched against her forehead, the tears seeping down her cold cheeks.

There was a silence in the room. The last chords quivered on the air and died away. Calum sat back, breathing heavily, as Rissa slowly raised her head and looked at him. He turned towards her, stiffly, as if he had been sitting there for a long time, and their glances met across the twilit room.

'So now you know,' he said heavily. 'That's what you're doing to me. That's how I feel. I call it *Tormented Rhapsody*.'

Rissa stared at him. '*That*—but I had no idea! Calum, I didn't know—I really didn't know——'

He got up and came over to her, taking her hands to draw her up against him, holding her close so that her breasts brushed against his body.

'Didn't you, Rissa? Didn't you really know? Had you no idea at all?'

'How could I?' she whispered, and felt herself tremble

in his arms. His hands slipped down from her wrists, fingertips moving gently down her bare arms, cupping her elbows, then moving to her waist. Rissa shivered. It was as if he was weaving a web around her so that she couldn't move; a web that was charged with a fine electricity, so that her whole body tingled. Her hands lay on his chest where he had brought them, and she let them move up to his shoulders, let them link themselves around his neck as Calum bent his head towards hers. This isn't happening, she thought confusedly. It *mustn't* happen. But her thoughts seemed to be detached from her body, which had apparently developed a will of its own and to be acting independently of her wishes. She felt herself move against him, delighting in the hardness of his body against her, and when his mouth touched hers at last she felt all her resistance ebb away, desire flooding through to take its place, and she met his lips with an eagerness that shook her and brought a groan from somewhere deep in his throat.

'*Rissa!*' he muttered against her mouth. 'Rissa, my— oh *God!*' And his kisses fired into passion, burning her cheeks, her eyes, her throat, searing down into the hollow between her breasts. His hands moved over her body, exploring its curves, holding her firmly against him, lifting her off her feet so that she had to cling to him in a sudden fear that they would fall. But Calum had no intention of falling; he let her slide slowly down his body and she gasped with the pleasure of it, reaching blindly up to repeat the sensation and squirming in her effort to get even closer.

She felt him lift her again, but this time he kept her in his arms as he moved across the room and laid her down on a wide couch. He knelt on the floor beside her, running his hand up and down the length of her body, letting his fingers stray and linger until she cried with tormented delight. His passion seemed more under control now; he was taking his time, letting them both savour every delicious moment, continually and steadily rousing Rissa's senses to a height she had never dreamed they could attain. But there could be even more; she knew that now and longed for it. And that climax was something Alistair would never be able to achieve for her, nor any other man. Only Calum. It was as if they had been together before; as if they were built for each other. And she pulled him closer, wanting to feel him against her from head to toe, wanting to know every tiny particle of him, while the music he had been playing still crashed through her head like a passionate accompaniment to their loving.

Then, so slowly that she didn't at first realise what he was doing, Calum gently brought her down from the heights, gradually easing the stimulation until at last she was calm and lay quietly in his arms. She felt her heartbeats slow down, felt the heat die away from her fevered body, and nestled her head against his shoulder as he cradled her like a child. But her mind was still spinning and she didn't understand. Why hadn't he gone on? They had both wanted it, she knew that now, and at last she had been willing. Why hadn't he taken advantage of the moment? And she felt for his mouth in the gathering darkness, tracing its lines with her finger and then drawing his head down to hers again in an attempt to rekindle the fire.

'Calum?' she whispered, and felt him smile against her fingers.

'It's all right, Rissa.' His arms tightened about her. 'I still want you—nothing's changed. And one day—one day soon, I hope—we'll get there. But I can't go all the way—not until you've made up your mind about Alistair.'

'Alistair?'

'Yes—Alistair, the man who's asked you to marry him, remember? I can't make love to you until you've given him your answer—and only then if the answer's no. You can see that, surely?'

A tiny chill entered Rissa's heart. So Calum was still prepared for her to marry another man. It *was* only an affair he wanted. Oh, his feelings were real enough—the music proved that. But this was as far as they went. An hour or two of delight on a warm summer evening. And then—nothing.

Somehow, the music and his passion after it had led her to expect something different. A commitment. His scruples over Alistair were no more than that—scruples over making love to another man's woman. Something that Calum presumably considered beyond his principles.

'So have you decided?' he murmured, letting his hand caress her body again from shoulder to knee, and Rissa shivered with the effort of not responding. She dared not respond—she knew that if she did she would be lost. And to be lost, while it thrilled her senses, also terrified that detached part of her mind which still looked on. An hour or two's delight, yes—fulfilment of a kind she would never again experience. And then—what? She couldn't risk it.

Alistair was her only protection. As long as Calum believed her to be thinking of marrying him, she would be safe. As safe as she could ever be. . . .

'No, I haven't decided,' she whispered. 'I've told him I'll think about it. It's the least I can do.'

'Think about it?' His hand moved on, covering the breast that swelled towards him. 'You'll think about it? What's there to think about, Rissa? Doesn't your body tell you—isn't it crying out its answer even now?' His fingers slipped inside her dress and she moaned softly as they found the smooth skin beneath, gently pinching the taut nipple. 'You can't fool me, Rissa. You never could. I've known how you felt ever since that first moment on the beach—and earlier than that. When you were too young for me to be able to do anything about it. You've always wanted me, Rissa, and you know it.'

'I was just a child,' she breathed, fighting the desire to submit to his caresses. 'I didn't know——'

'But you know now.' He had unfastened her bra and bent to kiss the rounded breast, letting his lips trail a path of fire across her heart. 'You know now. Does Alistair make you feel like this, Rissa? Does he kiss you like I do, touch you like I do? More important—do you kiss him as you kiss me——' his lips came up to hers and took them with an expertise that left her weak '—do you respond to him as you're responding to me now? Tell me the truth, Rissa, and then tell me if you're still *thinking* about his proposal—if you're thinking about him at all!'

Rissa moaned and moved her head from side to side. She wanted nothing more than for Calum to continue making love to her, to raise her to that pinnacle to which he had taken her a few minutes earlier, only to bring her down again. What did it matter about anything else? This was what was important—Calum and herself. Nothing else. . . .

Not now, perhaps, that little warning voice of detachment whispered in her ear. But how are you going to feel afterwards—when Calum has finished with you and you are totally committed to him?

'You know you only come fully alive when you're with me,' Calum's voice went on. 'Haven't you been told you're too serious—too responsible? Yet with me you blaze into life, even if it's only to be angry. Doesn't that mean anything? Doesn't it mean that we're two of a kind—that we *need* to be together, to——'

But Rissa could stand no more. With a sudden flash of clear sight, she knew that if she stayed here any longer she would be lost. She twisted sideways, out of Calum's arms, and scrambled off the end of the couch, evading his wild grab and putting a large mahogany table between them before he could get up and recapture her. For a moment she panted there, dazed and unable to do more than gaze at him. In that moment, Calum was on his feet and making for the table.

'No—don't touch me again, Calum! I couldn't bear it!'

'Couldn't bear it? What the hell do you mean? Don't

try to tell me that my touch revolts you, Rissa, because I know a whole lot better than that!'

'No, it doesn't revolt me,' she admitted. 'You know as well as I do that it's quite the reverse. But this isn't going to do either of us any good, Calum. I've told you about Alistair and you say you can't make love to me until I make up my mind. Are you playing fair in the way you're trying to convince me? You know what you're doing to me. Can't you leave me alone—at least until I've seen Alistair again?'

Calum ran his fingers through his hair, leaving it wild and disordered. 'I don't get it. Why do you need to see him? You know what your answer's going to be. You're not going to marry Alistair.'

His calm assumption angered her. 'And why not, pray? He's a fine man, he'll make me a good husband. He's kind and considerate, he's good company, we could be happy together——'

'Kind! Considerate! And are those the only qualities you look for in a husband?' he sneered.

'I think they're pretty good ones, don't you? Though I don't know why I should expect you to know anything about it,' she continued bitterly. 'You say you've never been in love or considered marriage——'

'Thank God!'

'—so you're not exactly an expert, are you?' she concluded. 'No, I don't think there's any advice you can give me in this situation, Calum. Perhaps when I need help in having a passionate affair one day I'll come to you. That's where your experience lies, isn't it!'

Calum said nothing. It was almost too dark now for her to see his face, but she could imagine exactly the expression that would be on it; grim, harsh, the severe lines drawing bitterness all over it. She shook her head wearily. This was getting them nowhere. In fact the whole encounter had only served to increase her frustration—and, presumably, his—and made it even more clear that there could never be any real commitment between them. The best thing would be to end it now.

'I think I ought to go home,' she said dully. 'It's late and I have to get up early tomorrow.' She turned towards the door. 'Can you lend me a torch to walk along the shore? It's quicker than by road.'

She half expected Calum to prevent her, but he seemed to have accepted at last her desire to be left alone. He shook his head impatiently and moved towards her.

'It's all right, you needn't cower away like that,' he said roughly. 'I shan't touch you again.' He moved to the door and flicked on a light, and they looked at each other in the sudden brightness. 'I'll take you home. I brought you here against your will, so it's only right.' He looked tired, she noticed, the lines of bitterness overlaid by fatigue, and for a moment she wanted to take him in her arms and comfort him—but it wouldn't do any good. Mutely, she followed him out of the door and back to the car.

Neither of them spoke as Calum drove the short distance back through the twisting lanes. Cluny Cottage was in darkness when they arrived, only a dim glow through the front door showing that Mandy had left a light on for her sister to come back. Calum stopped the car and reached across Rissa to open her door. His arm brushed her breasts as he did so and she stiffened, but it was as if he hadn't even noticed the contact. He said nothing as she got out, and she hesitated, not knowing what to say to him. But before she could make up her mind, he had let in the clutch and the car was moving forward, ready to turn round. And when he had done so and passed her again, his eyes looked straight ahead and he didn't even acknowledge the half-wave she gave him from the gate.

Rissa went up the little path to the front door and stood for a moment looking at the loch, at the silver pathway made by the weak light of the half-moon, at the dark bulk of the mountains on the far side. Somewhere over there was the ruined hut where she and Calum had spent a night together. Would she have been any happier now if she had allowed him to make love to her then? But it was silly to ask such questions; there was no way of knowing.

She unlocked the door and let herself into the cottage. It had been the strangest day she had ever spent, and she felt totally exhausted. Even more so because nothing had been decided or brought to any kind of conclusion. Her body ached with a restlessness that she knew must be caused by frustration. Was there no way to ease it?

Her sleep that night was disturbed by unhappy and unsatisfying dreams that left her more exhausted than ever. Several times she woke, convinced that Calum was there with her, ready to turn into his arms and give him all that love that she had for him. But each time her bed was empty. And, as far as she could tell, it always would be.

CHAPTER SIX

By the time Alistair was ready to return to Glasgow, Rissa knew that in fairness to him her answer must be no. She told him on their last evening together, as they walked together on the shore after supper. The moon was full now; it lit the mountains with a ghostly glow and turned the loch to silver. The shadows were black by contrast, and now and then a dozing waterbird would start up with a cry from its hiding-place in the rushes, splashing away across the water in needless panic.

When they were out of sight of Cluny Cottage, Alistair drew Rissa down on to the grass just above the beach. They sat together without speaking for a while, then he slipped his arm round her shoulders and gently turned her to face him.

'You've made up your mind, haven't you, Rissa?' he said quietly. 'You've had time to think, and you've decided. And I don't think I need ask what your decision is.'

Rissa looked at him and felt the tears in her eyes. 'I'm sorry, Alistair,' she whispered, and he nodded as if he had expected it.

'Well, I couldn't really believe I'd be so lucky. It's still Calum, isn't it?'

Rissa shrugged helplessly. 'It's so silly, Alistair. I know it'll never be any good—most of the time I wish we'd never met. But—I can't seem to help the way I feel, I——'

'I just wish I knew what he was playing at,' Alistair muttered. 'Making you miserable—spoiling your life. He needs horsewhipping!'

'No, it's not like that! You don't understand, Alistair—if I never saw Calum again I'd feel the same.

It isn't really his fault, it's just something between us, something neither of us can help. He probably feels the same—that it would have been better if we'd never met.'

'Well, I don't get it. You mean you'll never marry anyone, just because of this thing between you and Calum?'

Rissa's shoulders lifted. 'I honestly don't know. The way I feel at present—yes, that's what I mean. I can only hope it'll wear off.'

'And if it does?' Alistair gripped her shoulders and looked down intently into her eyes. 'Will you come to me then, Rissa? If you ever feel that you *could* marry me—will you come to me and tell me?'

'But I can't expect you to wait about on the offchance,' she objected, and he shook his head impatiently.

'I don't intend to! I don't share this view that there's only one man or woman in the world for anyone, Rissa. But I doubt if I'll find anyone else for quite a while—and if during that time you get over this fever for Calum and come to me, I'll be only too happy to get together again. So how about it?'

Well, at least he didn't sound brokenhearted, Rissa reflected a little ruefully. No protestations of undying love, no threats of not being able to live without her. And this promise was easy enough to make; she doubted if she would ever feel able to fulfil it, but in any case Alistair wasn't necessarily going to wait for her to do so. She smiled and nodded.

'All right, I promise. And—thank you for asking me, Alistair. A proposal from an attractive man can never be anything but good for a girl's morale. But I hope you do find someone else—one of those pretty nurses, perhaps? You're the sort who ought to be married.'

'And I'd have said the same about you,' said Alistair. He stood up and helped her to her feet. 'Well, we've both got early starts in the morning, so I guess we'd better be getting back.' He looked down at her and rested his hands lightly on her waist. 'I've enjoyed this holiday,' he said seriously. 'Washing-up and all! And—well, I'm not going to indulge in any hysterics, Rissa, but I did mean what I said. I still think we could make a go of it, and if you do change your mind. . . .'

'Thanks, Alistair,' she said softly. 'I'll remember.' And she reached up to give him a kiss. 'I only wish things could have been different. And I'll tell you one thing—any girl who does find herself walking down the aisle with you will be a very lucky girl indeed. Just send her to me if she's got any doubts!'

Without Alistair, Cluny Cottage seemed a quieter place, and the two girls settled down into a routine. There was plenty to do as the season advanced, and it was soon clear that they needed help for at least part of the time; they engaged a girl from the village to come in and help during the mornings and lunchtimes, while Rissa was busy in the kitchen cooking and preparing salads, and an older woman to help at weekends and on Mondays and Tuesdays when Rissa and Mandy took it in turns to have a day off. Paying the extra wages made their budget a little tighter than they had planned for, but it was obvious that without the extra help the tea-room would have been less efficient, and Rissa was anxious to build up a good name.

She saw little of Calum. He seemed to have become something of a recluse at Kilvanie; coming within earshot of the long white house on her evening walks before she went to bed, she would hear the sound of the piano drifting on the still air, and once she recognised the tormented strains of the rhapsody he had played to her. Abruptly, she turned and walked back the other way; but the next evening found herself walking there again, though she had made up her mind to avoid Calum if he appeared. But he never did appear, and her only glimpses of him were at the wheel of his car, driving through the village, and once in the distance, walking high up on the shoulder of the hills.

The holiday season was well under way and the tea-room running smoothly when Rissa returned from her afternoon off one Monday to find Mandy waiting in the garden, her small face glowing with excitement.

'Guess what!' she exclaimed as soon as Rissa came within earshot. 'Guess who's here?'

Rissa's heart gave a leap, then settled. It couldn't be Calum! Mandy would have taken this visit for granted. She hoped it wasn't Alistair. She had heard from him twice since he'd gone back to Glasgow, friendly, affectionate letters that had been easy to reply to. Who else could it be?

'*Alison!*' Mandy told her gleefully. 'Isn't it lovely? She just decided on the spur of the moment to pay us a visit, and here she is! She arrived this afternoon.'

Alison! Rissa hurried towards the cottage, wondering what had caused this sudden visit. She hadn't seen her stepsister for over two years, and then only briefly. In fact they hadn't had much contact since that summer holiday here at Ichrachan seven years ago. What could have brought her back? She couldn't have very happy memories of the place, after the unhappiness of her affair with Calum. Rissa had had a strong impression then that she never wanted to see Cluny Cottage again.

She went into the big, shabby kitchen. Alison was there, sitting back in the battered old sofa, looking as out of place as a tropical butterfly on a cabbage patch. Her long slim legs gleamed under the skirt of a dove-grey suede suit, the jacket of which was open to reveal a silk blouse of glowing apricot. Glittering diamonds in her ears matched the slender watch on her wrist, and her hair fell in a shining cloud almost to her shoulders.

'Alison!' Rissa exclaimed. 'What a surprise!'

'Hi, Rissa,' the American girl drawled. 'Yeah, I guess it is. You know me, though—make up my mind to do a thing and I *do* it. And after Mom had told me all about what you were doing up here I just had to come along and see for myself.'

'How *is* Kate?' asked Rissa, settling herself in an armchair and accepting a mug of coffee from Mandy. 'And how long can you stay? It's lovely to see you again—you don't have to rush away too soon, do you?'

'Well, I haven't made any firm plans. Guess I'll just see which way the wind blows me.' Alison's perfect teeth showed in a smile. 'But tell me all about yourselves and what you're doing. I just love what you've done to Cluny—it's real neat. Is it doing well? Are you making lots and lots of money?'

'Well, I wouldn't say that,' Rissa laughed. 'We're making a living—of sorts. But there's not a lot to spend money on up here, fortunately, and we both love being here. And of course we've so many old friends here that it's really like coming home.'

'Yeah, Mandy's been telling me.' Alison studied her grey suede shoes. 'You've got your resident genius here at present too, I understand—Calum Kilmartin. Still wowing them in the concert halls, is he?'

Rissa looked at her attentively. Surely she couldn't be interested in Calum—not after all this time? But Alison's face was as casual as her voice, as if she wasn't really interested in the answer to her question and had only asked it for something to say.

'Yes, he's at Kilvanie just now,' Rissa said noncommittally. 'He composes too, you know. I think he's working on a new piano concerto.'

'And Alistair too,' Alison went on. 'I hear I've just missed him—that's a shame. But I'll get to see Donald, won't I? Mandy tells me he's settling here for good.'

'Yes, that's right.' Rissa spoke briefly, not wanting to start another argument with Mandy at this point. They continued to discuss old acquaintances and she was surprised to find how much Alison remembered of their friends at Ichrachan. Then, having exhausted the subject, they passed on to Alison's own life and this, it seemed, she was happy to talk about for as long as her listeners liked.

'And what about men?' asked Rissa after a lengthy

description of modelling in New York. 'Don't tell me you haven't got a string of admirers!'

Alison laughed. 'Well, I have to admit that there are just a few! Actually, there's been one man for quite a while now—Maxwell. He's—he was—pretty special.' She frowned at her perfectly-manicured fingernails. 'But we split up recently. He was getting too possessive.' Her tone was abrupt and Rissa guessed that she didn't want to talk about it. Perhaps this was the reason for her sudden visit to Scotland. She evidently felt the split more than she cared to reveal.

A thought struck her. 'Has Mandy done anything about a room for you?' she asked, starting to get out of her chair. 'The spare room's rather crowded, I'm afraid—we keep our stores up there—but you could have my room and I'll move into it——'

'Relax,' Mandy ordered, pushing her back into the chair. 'I've swapped over myself. Alison's all fixed. There's nothing for you to do but sit back and enjoy yourself.'

So Rissa did just that. Although when the evening had ended and she found herself alone in the bedroom overlooking the loch, she found herself wondering just what the change was in Alison. She seemed different, somehow. More assured than ever—more poised and sophisticated, though she'd been those things before. Was she just a little harder? Rissa didn't like to think that; but maybe if you were a model in New York and had just split up with a man who was 'pretty special' you might find yourself becoming harder. If you didn't, you probably didn't survive.

Of course, the change might be in herself. She had been little more than a child when Alison had been here last, and their meetings since had been both brief and infrequent. How well had she really known Alison?

She got into bed and sat there for a while, gazing thoughtfully out at the loch. One thing was certain. Ichrachan, with its wild hills and lack of modern facilities and entertainments, wasn't likely to interest the beautiful and sophisticated American girl for very long. No doubt this visit too would turn out to be brief. And just at the moment Rissa wasn't sure whether to be glad or sorry.

It was Mandy's turn to have a day off the next day, and while preparing to take Alison's breakfast up to her, she announced her intention of asking the older girl to spend the day with her and Donald. 'We're taking the boat up the loch with some of the hotel guests,' she explained, arranging a few rambling roses from the garden in a small glass on Alison's tray. 'It's going to be a lovely day—should be fun.'

'I'm not at all sure Alison will want to come, though,' Rissa warned her. 'She doesn't strike me as the outdoor type, and if all her clothes are as super as that suede suit she had on yesterday she won't be too keen on messing about in boats.'

'Oh, she's bound to have some older things with her,' Mandy said confidently. 'After all, she's been here before. There! Doesn't that look nice?'

'Very nice,' Rissa agreed dryly, wondering what it was about Alison that made people want to wait on her. 'Well, I'd better get started or we shan't be opening at ten-thirty. And Esme will be here soon.'

Mandy went upstairs and came back to report that Alison had accepted her invitation and would be ready by the time Donald wanted to start off. A faint surprise crossed Rissa's mind at this—she was sure she remembered Alison refusing to go on any boat trips when she had been here before—but seven years was a long time, and people did change. Anyway, it was a relief to have Alison taken care of for the day. With Mandy away, Rissa would have been too busy to entertain the visitor, and she couldn't see Alison rolling up her sleeves and tackling the washing-up as Alistair had done.

Left alone in the cottage after the other two had gone—Alison dressed now in what she clearly imagined to be a practical boating outfit of bright green silky culottes and a dazzlingly colourful shirt tied just under her breasts to reveal a tanned midriff—Rissa drifted to the window and gazed out at the loch. The early morning mist had not entirely evaporated and fragile wisps still lay like gossamer on the surface of the pearly water. The tide was running up the loch, as it had been on the day of her canoeing trip, and she stifled a sigh as she thought of that day. It seemed that her relationship with Calum was just a long catalogue of wasted opportunities, and she smiled wryly at the thought that Alison would certainly have handled the whole thing better. But then Alison had learned in a hard school, hadn't she; she too had been hurt by Calum. And that, Rissa decided, wasn't an experience one easily forgot.

With her mind still on Calum, wondering just what he was doing and feeling now and how much longer he intended to stay in the glen, she turned away from the window. Esme wasn't due for half an hour, but she might as well make a start on the salads for lunch. She went out to the little outhouse, once a wash-house, where they kept the vegetables—and, coming out with an armful of lettuces, gave a start and dropped the lot.

'*Calum!* You—you scared me.' Flustered, feeling the hot colour swamp her cheeks, she bent and began gathering them up again. 'You shouldn't lurk behind doors like that,' she accused, her voice shaking. 'You might give someone a heart attack!'

'In your case, that's a pretty fair description of what I hope I am giving you,' he said tersely, making no attempt to help her. 'I take it you're alone here? It *is* Mandy's day off, isn't it?'

'Yes, it is. But Esme will be coming soon and I've got a lot——'

'What I want to say won't take long.' He followed her into the kitchen. 'Put those lettuces down, Rissa. I can't talk to you while you're holding them up like a barricade.'

Reluctantly, realising that this was just how she had been using them, Rissa laid the lettuces on the worktop and eyed Calum warily. Her heart was hammering and her legs felt weak, but she tilted her chin and hoped these effects didn't show. She had made up her mind that there could be no future for her with Calum, and she didn't want him to touch her, because she knew if he did resistance would be very difficult indeed.

'Did you come for anything special, Calum?' she asked, and saw his eyes narrow.

'You're damn right I did, and you know what it is, too! I've been waiting for you, Rissa. Alistair's been back in Glasgow for—what is it now? Two weeks, three?—and I expected you to come and tell me whether or not you'd agreed to marry him. But you haven't been near me, so——'

Rissa gasped. The sheer arrogant effrontery of it! 'No, I *haven't* been near you!' she exclaimed. 'And why should I? What's between Alistair and me has nothing at all to do with you——'

'*Hasn't* it? I thought it had a very great deal to do with me——'

'Well, it hasn't! Oh, I know what you said—that you couldn't make love to me if I was going to marry Alistair. But did *I* say that I wanted you to?'

'You didn't have to,' he murmured silkily, moving towards her. 'Your body said it all.'

'Well, it's not saying it again,' she retorted, skipping out of his reach. 'All right, Calum, I admit it's there, this chemistry you talk about, but that doesn't mean I *want* you to make love to me. I don't, and I'm not giving you the chance again. So just——'

'You still haven't answered me,' he interrupted, and she saw with a tremor of fear that he was now between her and the door. 'Are you going to marry Alistair or not?'

'I'm not telling you!' Oh, why couldn't Esme arrive early for once? 'I still say it's none of your business, and as long as you have these so-called scruples of yours I'm not saying a word.'

'In other words, no. Or you'd be only too eager to

tell me.' His eyes were like gimlets. 'I wonder why. He was going to be such a perfect husband. Good company, you said, kind, considerate. I wonder why those things shouldn't be enough?'

Rissa felt her cheeks flame and turned away abruptly. 'I told you, it's none of your business.'

'All the same, it's only natural that I should wonder.' He moved nearer and she looked wildly round for escape. 'But maybe I know the answer anyway. Do you think that's possible, Rissa? Do *you* think I know the answer?' He was close now, almost touching her, and as Rissa drew in her breath she smelt the fresh masculine tang of his after-shave. She stood perfectly still, almost as if paralysed, unable either to move or protest as he reached out his hand and let his fingers trail softly, lingeringly, down her cheek, down the slim column of her neck, and hover in the little hollow between her breasts. She closed her eyes, fighting the faintness, the almost overwhelming desire to move into his arms and lay her head on the broad chest. She had lain naked against that chest once, she thought, and her mind reeled at the memory. But even so, she managed to retain her hold, however tenuously, on the decision she had made.

'Stay away from me, Calum,' she said, and her voice was a mere thread. 'I've told you, there's nothing doing. I may not be going to marry Alistair, but that doesn't make me yours. *I don't want to be your mistress, Calum Kilmartin!*'

'Who said anything about being my mistress?' he murmured, closing in and sliding his arms around her. His head bent to hers and his lips brushed hers with a gentleness that made her want to cry out. 'I want you to——'

But what he was about to say was lost. As Rissa's eyes opened and she stared up at him, her heart threshing with sudden excitement, the kitchen door burst open. *Oh no, not Esme now!* she thought, forgetting that a few minutes ago she was wishing her helper would arrive early. And she jerked away from Calum as if they had been caught committing a crime.

But it wasn't Esme. It was Alison. Alison, looking exotic and outlandish in her tropical-printed outfit, her blonde hair artistically windswept, her eyes shining as she stood there gazing at them. Alison, her lips parted in speculation as she took in Calum's appearance in his dark-blue slacks and grey silk shirt, and moved forward with a practised smile already forming on her lips and both hands held out.

There was no trace there of the girl who had come in white-faced seven years ago and made it clear that she wasn't seeing Calum again. This was an attractive woman meeting an attractive man and already working out the possibilities. And from the look on Calum's face, after that split second of surprise, he wasn't far behind.

'Alison!' Rissa said faintly. 'I wasn't expecting you back. . . .'

'I don't suppose you were.' Her tone was enigmatic, and Rissa flushed. Had Alison actually seen them, seen Calum about to kiss her? Or had they jumped apart before she came through the door? In any case, she couldn't have any real doubt about what had been happening. It still vibrated in the air.

'Calum——' Alison had turned back to him, both her small, shapely hands in Calum's large ones '—it's just wonderful to see you again! How *are* you? They tell me you're a big success now. Well, I always knew you would be. Remember those days, Calum? When you used to play to me and I used to curl up in that big old sofa and listen? Have you still got that sofa?'

'Not now.' He was smiling down at her. 'But I've got another, even bigger and comfier. Haven't I, Rissa?'

Rissa felt her cheeks redden again, remembering the way he had laid her in it, the way he had knelt beside her and caressed her. She caught Alison's sharp glance and turned away quickly. The American girl was too knowing, she saw far too much, and Rissa didn't want to expose her feelings to that assessing gaze.

But Alison wasn't really interested in her. She was too engrossed in Calum, her smile inviting him to remember *her* on the sofa. Giving his hands a little shake, she reached up and kissed him, looping her arms round his neck and nuzzling his cheek afterwards. And Calum didn't seem in any hurry to break the embrace. He held her wrist, smiling down at her in a way he never smiled at Rissa.

'Isn't this *fun*?' Alison cried, still keeping her arms round his neck. 'Look, Calum, I just came back for a waterproof, Donald says it could be wet in the boat even if it doesn't rain—we're going up the loch. Why don't you come with us? There's room for another one, and there's plenty of lunch provided.' She tugged playfully at his thick black hair. 'Say you'll come, Cal, there's a sweetie!'

He won't fall for *that*, Rissa told herself, picking up a lettuce and slicing viciously through its stem. Calum hated crowds, especially on the water. But to her astonishment, as she turned away, she heard his deep, measured tones say with every semblance of pleasure: 'That's a good idea, Alison. I'd enjoy it, and I'm due for a day off. Look, I'll come down to the boat with you right away and Donald can stop off at Kilvanie jetty to let me collect some more suitable clothes—all right?'

'That's just great,' Alison told him enthusiastically. 'Rissa, can *you* find me a waterproof? Mandy did tell me where, but in all the excitement I've forgotten.' She watched as Rissa went upstairs without a word, and as Rissa searched out an anorak—choosing the shabbiest she could find—she could hear Alison's voice running on downstairs. She doesn't mean me to be alone with him, Rissa thought bitterly, not for one moment. But she needn't have bothered—I'm only too pleased that we were interrupted. And if she wants to take up where she left off with Calum Kilmartin, then she's welcome too. At least it'll keep his mind off me!

But the feeling that had been growing in her ever

since she watched Alison reach up to kiss Calum a few minutes ago kept on growing as she handed over the anorak and watched the two figures—so well suited, one with black hair, the other with blonde—walk away down the path. She was too dazed to take in quite what had happened, it had all been so quick. And there wasn't time to think about it now, as Esme was hurrying along the lane ready to start the day's work, and it would soon be time to open.

But the feeling stayed with her all day. A grey, leaden lump of misery, deep in her stomach; shot through with a searing pain whenever she recalled the kiss Alison and Calum had shared, and the way he had held her in his arms and looked down with pleasure into her lovely, tilted face.

The day dragged by. There were plenty of customers and Rissa was kept busy, but her mind was never more than half at the tea-room. Most of it was in the boat, chugging up the loch with Donald at the helm telling his passengers about the mountains on either side, making them crane their necks for a sight of the golden eagle that cruised like a black speck high above the peaks. Mandy would be beside Donald, she knew, her black hair blowing in the breeze, absolutely at home in her faded jeans and old sweater. And Calum and Alison? No doubt they would be sitting together too, Calum's strong arm enclosing the glamorous American girl, laughing into each other's faces, moving closer to feel the touch of each other's bodies. . . .

Rissa snapped her mind away from the picture she had conjured up. It did no good to think like that, she scolded herself. And what was the matter with her anyway? She *wanted* Calum to forget her, didn't she? She *wanted* him to leave her alone. And what better distraction than Alison, the kind of girl who would turn any man's head, the girl he had already had one affair with and maybe even hankered for all these years. He had never married, never had a serious romance. Could it be that now Alison had come back into his life all that would change?

All the same, she did wish she knew what it was he had been about to say when Alison had burst in on them. She had a feeling it had been something important. And she had a stronger feeling that she would never hear it, now.

It was late in the evening before anyone returned, and then it was Mandy, alone. She looked bright and happy, her small face sunburnt from the long day on the water, and she came in with Alison's borrowed anorak and dropped it on a chair.

'Had a good day?' asked Rissa, steeling herself not to ask about Alison.

'Mm, lovely. We went right up to the head of the loch and landed at the pier, and spent the afternoon there. Some people walked quite a way up into the hills. Donald and I went swimming under the waterfall, it was marvellous. And we saw the eagle, too.' She frowned slightly. 'Rissa, why ever did you give Alison that old anorak? It's in a dreadful state. *My* old one's better than that!'

'It was the first one I came across,' Rissa said vaguely. 'Um—is Alison coming?'

'Not yet, she went back to Kilvanie with Calum. We dropped them at the jetty, that's why I brought her anorak. She and Calum get on well, don't they? I thought they'd had an argument of some kind, years ago. Seems to be all forgotten now, though.'

'Want anything to eat?' Rissa asked, unable to comment on that remark. Mandy shook her head.

'No, I had something at the hotel, with Donald. Oh, Alison asked me to tell you she's invited Calum to dinner tomorrow evening. And Donald. She says not to worry, she'd do everything, she'll go into Oban in the morning and get things and she'll get it all ready herself. Should be fun, shouldn't it? She's asked Donald too, of course.'

'I . . . see.' Rissa felt as if the wind had been taken

out of her sails. Of course, there was no reason to take offence. It was nice of Alison to offer to get the meal. But somehow she felt 'taken over'. And the lump of misery that had lain in her stomach all day grew heavier still. 'I think I'll go to bed,' she said, knowing that she couldn't stand any more talk about Alison that evening. 'I suppose Alison didn't say what time she'd be in?'

'No, she didn't.' Mandy was picking up the anorak again. 'Only that she'd probably be rather late.'

And so she was. Rissa had been lying awake for several hours when she finally heard the soft purr of Calum's sleek grey car stop outside Cluny Cottage. And it didn't take much imagination, she thought miserably, to know what had been going on at Kilvanie all that time. . . .

The morning was well advanced when Alison got up, coming downstairs yawning to the kitchen where Rissa and Mandy were snatching a quick cup of coffee between customers. She looked sleepy and maddeningly contented, Rissa thought, and naturally as glamorous as ever in a silky housecoat that clung seductively to her perfect figure. She sat down at the kitchen table and accepted the coffee Rissa handed her.

'I sure hope I didn't disturb you last night,' she drawled. 'It was pretty late when Cal brought me home.'

'No, not at all,' Rissa said politely. 'Did——' she swallowed, wishing she hadn't begun this particular question '—did you have a good time?'

'Oh, fan*ta*stic.' Alison stretched slender arms above her head. 'Cal sure is one hell of a guy. He's developed a *lot* since the last time we met. Oh, did Mandy tell you I'd asked him here tonight? I hope you don't mind— only I wanted to cook a meal for him myself, you know how it is. I thought I'd take the car into the nearest town—Oban, isn't it?—and pick up a few things. Then I can get on with the preparation during the afternoon.'

'Yes, that's all right.' There wasn't much else she

could say, after all. But the delight with which she
had welcomed Alison only two days ago seemed to
have faded, and she wondered just how long the older
girl planned to stay. As long as Calum, probably, she
thought with a tinge of bitterness, and was relieved
when Mandy noticed some more customers coming
up the path and she was able to hurry out to
welcome them.

Alison left soon after that, wearing her suede suit
again and driving the little car she had hired at the
airport. She didn't return for lunch, but appeared
towards the middle of the afternoon laden with bags
and parcels and smilingly refusing all Mandy's offers of
help to carry them in.

'This meal is going to be a surprise,' she declared,
'and from now on the kitchen's out of bounds.'

'Sorry, but that's impossible,' Rissa told her shortly.
'You must see we have to be in and out the whole time.
Anyway, we won't have much time to look, so you
needn't worry.'

'Hey, Rissa, you don't need to get so uptight,' Alison
protested, looking at her with amusement. 'I guess
you're tired, though. Running a place like this must be
pretty strenuous at times. Okay, I'll try to keep out of
your way. You just forget I'm there.'

'Chance would be a fine thing,' Rissa muttered as
Alison went through to the kitchen, and Mandy glanced
at her curiously.

'What's the matter, Rissa? Don't you like having
Alison here? You were quite rude then, you know.'

'Oh, she's all right.' Rissa collected up some dirty
cups, moving restlessly. 'Don't take any notice of me,
Mandy. She's probably right, I'm just tired—but it does
seem an awful lot more bother having someone else in
the house.'

'You didn't mind Alistair, and he practically lived
here for a fortnight,' Mandy remarked.

'Alistair was different.'

'Well, you can't expect Alison to spend her holiday

washing up and washing lettuces. She could do that at home.'

'No, I know. Oh, forget it, Mandy. I'm just in a bad mood.'

A bad mood which increased during the afternoon, as every time Rissa came into the kitchen she found Alison there, gradually taking up more and more of the workspace and apparently intent on using every utensil in the place. Fortunately, Rissa had invested in a good many labour-saving appliances so was saved the humiliation of not being able to provide whatever Alison demanded, but she was aware of the American girl's disparaging glances at what she probably considered outdated equipment.

At last it was time to close the tea-room, which Rissa did more thankfully than ever before, and she went upstairs feeling more than ready to sink into a hot bath. But—she might have known it, she thought, uselessly twisting the handle—Alison, finished at last in the kitchen, was there first. And somehow Rissa knew that she was going to be there for a long, long time.

Oh, why don't you just go and *live* with the man, she thought bitterly as she turned away. You're more than welcome to him, in fact, you're welcome to each other!

'You're looking awfully fed up,' Mandy remarked, coming out of her own room just then. 'You know what I think is the matter? You're missing Alistair!'

'I am *not* missing Alistair!' Rissa snapped, ignoring her sister's look of astonishment at her unusual bad temper. 'I'm not missing *anybody*. In fact, that's the whole trouble—there are altogether *too many* people about!' And she went into her room and shut the door, hard.

It was, as she had suspected, some time before Alison came out of the bathroom, and then before Rissa could scramble up from the bed where she had been lying, she heard Mandy go in. Oh, what the hell, she thought wearily, sinking back again. I just won't hurry. It doesn't matter if I'm not down when Calum arrives

anyway—it's not me he's coming to see. And no doubt
Alison will be all the better pleased if I *am* late. It'll give
her all the more time alone with him.

And what if it does, a cold little voice inside her
asked. What does it matter to you? You don't want
him—or do you? Could it be—could it just be—that
you're jealous?

The thought struck at her like an arrow. *Jealous?*
No—never. She wasn't the jealous type. And she'd
already made up her mind about Calum. She'd rejected
him—or tried to. She couldn't resent his liking someone
else.

But you love him, don't you? the little voice persisted.
And that's really all that matters.

And with a groan, Rissa admitted that it was.

She was, as she had foreseen, last to arrive in the tea-
room where Alison had insisted on serving the meal.
('In the *kitchen*?' she had echoed when Rissa observed
that that was where they usually ate. 'Oh, *no*, Rissa!')
She had been down there for some time, Rissa knew,
rearranging the furniture to suit herself, and Rissa had
to admit that it did look very attractive. Several tables
had been pulled together to make one large one and a
big tablecloth had been spread over them all. A wide,
low arrangement of flowers held pride of place in the
centre, and four tall candles burned steadily around
them. The flickering light brought mysterious shadows
into the room she knew so well and changed its
character completely. Rissa found herself wondering
about opening in the evenings—serving candlelit
dinners. Would there be much call for that kind of
thing in Ichrachan? There was the hotel already, but—

Her thoughts were interrupted by Calum, who was
sitting at one of the windows, half hidden by the
shadows. He was watching her in amusement, Rissa
thought, and immediately felt plain and dowdy. She
had put on an ordinary dress, quite attractive but
nothing special, knowing that whatever she wore Alison
would outshine her; but now she wished she had tried

harder. It was the effect Alison had on her—to make her behave childishly. Like picking out the shabbiest anorak and sulking because she couldn't get into the bathroom. . . .

'I'm sorry. What did you say?' she asked politely, realising too late that they were the only ones in the room, Mandy and Donald being in the garden while Alison put the final touches to the meal. Calum's teeth flashed and he repeated his remark.

'I said, it seems that Alison believes there's something to celebrate. What do you suppose it is? Her return to the glens or something else?'

'I wouldn't know,' Rissa said woodenly, conscious of a pain somewhere around her heart. 'We haven't really had a great deal of time to talk.'

'Meaning I have?' His eyes glittered in the flickering light and he looked even more devastatingly handsome than usual. Like a devil—a devil, come to torment her. 'You don't look your usual self tonight, Rissa. What's the matter? Things not going your way for once?'

'You talk as if I'm a spoilt child,' she flashed, lifting her head.

'Well, aren't you?' Oh, that maddening calm! 'Isn't that just what you've always been? Oh, not in the material sense, perhaps—but in other ways, haven't you always had things just the way you wanted them? I seem to remember that it was always Rissa who led the pack, Rissa who decided what the day's activities would be. Rissa who took charge when Mrs Loring died——'

'That's a horrible thing to say! I *had* to—who else was there? I had to look after Mandy and Dad—and I was only twelve, remember!'

'Oh, I remember,' he said softly. 'Everyone said what a good little mother you were to Mandy, didn't they? What a wonderful help to your father. Taking on all that responsibility at such a tender age. And you liked that, didn't you? You liked feeling capable and collecting all the admiration. Most of all——' he uncoiled and came out of the chair like a snake about to strike '—most of all you liked being in charge. As you still do. Look at the way you're trying to run Mandy's life! And that——' he came closer, while Rissa stared at him like a hypnotised rabbit '—is why you're indulging in this fit of the sulks now, dear Rissa. Because someone else is getting the attention. Someone else is in charge—and in *your* domain, too—the kitchen! What could be worse?'

Rissa glared at him. 'You're just being sarcastic and horrible! There's not a grain of truth in what you say——'

'No? Not a grain?' His big hand came up and tilted her chin so that she had to meet his eyes. 'Think about it, Rissa. I think you'll find there is—and more than a grain, at that. But I can hear the others coming in— we'll save the rest of this conversation for later, shall we?'

Not if I have anything to do with it, Rissa thought rebelliously, moving away from him. Not later, not *ever*. And she deliberately turned her back on Calum to greet Donald with such warmth that he blinked in surprise.

After that, the evening went more or less as she had pictured it, with Alison enlisting Mandy's help in serving the food—an odd mixture of sweet things and savoury, Rissa thought, wondering just what Calum was making of the various meats in their sauces; if she remembered rightly, he was very much a plain eater, enjoying a good old-fashioned roast or steak-and-kidney pudding more than any fancy meal. But it seemed that he had changed even in that. He ate the meal with every appearance of relish and sitting back at the end with a more than satisfied smile on his face.

'Well done, Alison,' he congratulated her. 'You must have worked really hard to produce that meal. Not often we get cooking like that in this part of the world, is it, Donald? You'll have to offer Alison a job at the hotel!'

'Aye, I'll tell Dad.' Donald's pleasant smile flashed in

the candlelight. 'And now, Alison, you're not to do a scrap more work. Mandy and I'll tidy the room for you, and then give Rissa a hand with the washing up. Why don't you and Calum take a walk down the shore before it gets dark?'

'Sounds a good idea,' observed Calum, getting to his feet while Alison hesitated prettily. 'Come on, Alison. These folk are more at home around the kitchen than we are—for washing up, anyway.'

Alison smiled round at them. 'Well, if you're really sure. You know, I'm getting thoroughly spoilt here. If this goes on, why, I just won't want to leave at all!'

Rissa remained silent until the door had closed behind them. Then she flung down her napkin and exploded. '*Spoilt!* I'll say she is, I've never seen anyone so spoilt in all my life! And *him*—saying we're more at home with the washing up! There's one good way to cure that—but you won't catch Miss America at the sink with a mop in her hand. No, *she's* more at home setting her cap at the men. And you needn't look like that, Donald—if it hadn't been for Calum she'd have been after you, I've no doubt at all. Anything in trousers will do for that one!'

'I'll wear my kilt next time, then,' Donald said mildly. 'Honestly, Rissa, I think you're exaggerating a bit. Why shouldn't she see something of Calum? They were good friends once. And it keeps him out of your hair, doesn't it?'

'And just what do you mean by that?' Rissa snapped, so fiercely that he took a step back.

'He doesn't mean anything,' exclaimed Mandy, coming to his rescue. 'Only what anyone with half an eye can see for themselves. You and Calum strike sparks off each other every time you meet. Everything you say to each other is barbed. *You* obviously can't stand the sight of him—so why should you mind if Alison can?' With quick, angry movements she began to clear the table. 'I don't know what's come over you, Rissa. I thought it was going to be such fun being here

with you, and instead——' her voice broke '—instead
you're like a bear with a sore head. I don't know what's
wrong, but I wish you'd snap out of it!'

Rissa bit her lip. Mandy was right, but there didn't
seem to be a thing she could do about it. Silently, she
stacked a pile of plates and carried them through to the
kitchen. It was almost dark there, with no lights on, but
outside dusk hadn't fully fallen and she could see down
to the shore where Alison and Calum walked, Calum
with his arm round the American girl's waist to prevent
her from stumbling in her high heels. At least, that was
what Rissa would have liked to think; but as she
watched, the two stopped walking and turned to each
other. Their figures were like shadows in the gloaming;
they came together and merged, a single, united shadow
silhouetted against the pale waters of the loch. And they
were still there, still merged and motionless, when Rissa
put down the plates, turned and went blindly up the
stairs, leaving Mandy and Donald to clear up all by
themselves.

CHAPTER SEVEN

AFTER that night, Rissa was forced to admit to herself that she loved and wanted Calum so much that had he come to her then she would have given in to him—or rather, to herself. But it didn't seem as if the chance would arise again. Alison now had first claim on his time, and it seemed that he was quite happy to have it so. So it was just chemistry after all, as far as he was concerned, Rissa thought wretchedly. Love really had never entered into it, never would. She wondered again what he had been about to say when Alison had first interrupted them. Probably that he didn't even want any such long-term relationship as a mistress—just a one-night stand, to get the fever from his blood. Well, he didn't need to do that now. Alison was clearly prepared to do all the cooling-down that might be necessary.

'Oh, by the way, I won't be here for a couple of days,' Alison announced one morning as she sat drinking her coffee while Rissa and Mandy hurried in and out with trays. 'Calum's taking me to Edinburgh. He has to see some people about the Festival and thought I'd like the trip.'

'I see.' It made a good excuse, anyway, Rissa thought. Aloud, she asked: 'Will you be staying here until the Festival?'

'Oh, I guess so—must hear Calum's new composition. He's going to be playing, too, of course. It'll be quite an event.'

'Yes, it will.' Rissa wondered if *Tormented Rhapsody* would be part of his concerto. 'When are you going for this trip, then? Tomorrow?'

'Mm.' Alison drank her coffee. 'Why, here he is now. He can tell you all about it.'

Thankfully, Rissa saw that Calum's arrival had coincided with that of a large group of hearty young Dutchmen who were disgorging themselves from a minibus (first of the coaches, she thought with a tinge of malicious delight that he should be there to witness it) and she made her escape to go and serve them. With any luck, Calum should have gone, taking Alison with him, by the time she had finished with them, and by then there might be more customers anyway. But apart from a lone walker nobody else came during the next half-hour, and when she had served the cheerful Dutchmen with coffee and a huge plate of scones and cakes, she returned to the kitchen to find Calum very much at his ease and Alison pouring more coffee, while Mandy washed up.

'You're off to Edinburgh, I hear,' she said, keeping her tone cool though the sight of him still did strange things to her heart.

'That's right. Taking Alison to see the sights. Why don't you come, too, Rissa? You could do with a couple of days off—you're looking tired. Mandy could cope, with Esme and young Fiona, couldn't she?'

Rissa stared at him. Just what was he playing at? He had hardly taken any notice of her since Alison had arrived—even though he had spent more time than ever before at Cluny Cottage. All his attention had been focussed on the American girl and she had quite obviously revelled in it. Even Mandy had begun to notice her blatant determination to capture him.

'Come to Edinburgh?' she repeated. 'Oh, I couldn't— we're too busy, and——'

'Of course you could,' Mandy put in, emerging from the kitchen extension with a tea-towel in her hands. 'We could manage perfectly well. Donald would help. And Calum's right, you *do* need a break. You've been looking quite strained lately.'

Tired—strained—why didn't they just come out with it and say she looked plain old and haggard? Especially beside Alison! Helplessly, Rissa glanced at her stepsister and saw exactly what she had expected—an expression of cold anger and, quite definitely, a warning. *She* wasn't adding to the invitation, and once again Rissa wondered just what Calum was playing at.

'Look, it's out of the question,' she tried again, for once sympathising with Alison. Two was company, after all! 'There's the baking, I do all of that——'

'But you don't *have* to,' Mandy broke in again. 'I'm getting better now—I can make scones and flapjacks—if we had a couple of evenings hard at it, with you doing the other things, we could freeze enough to last a couple of days, surely? Honestly, Rissa, we could manage——'

'Not if it means doing that,' Rissa told her triumphantly. 'Calum wants to go tomorrow.'

'Oh, it doesn't have to be tomorrow,' he drawled, a gleam of pure wickedness in his eyes. 'We can make it the day after—that'll give you time to get organised, won't it? And I know Alison won't mind.'

Do you? Rissa thought, unable to suppress a twitch of amusement at the look on Alison's face. But there was nothing either she or the American girl could say; both were caught in the same trap. Rissa shrugged and gave in, though she couldn't see any of them actually enjoying the trip.

'All right, I'll come—the day after tomorrow. But I must be back the next night—I can't leave Mandy to cope by herself any longer than that.'

'You worry too much,' Mandy told her, but she went back to her washing up with a smile. Rissa glanced uncertainly at the other two. Calum was pouring himself more coffee, a secret smile pulling at his mobile lips, and refused to return her glance. Alison was obviously seething, her full mouth sulky and her eyes stormy. Whether she would actually voice her protest to Calum once they were alone was anybody's guess. But Rissa couldn't see her leaving him in any doubt as to her feelings. The romantic little jaunt to Edinburgh, which she had taken pleasure in waving under Rissa's nose, wasn't going to be at all the same now.

But Rissa would still have liked to know just what was in Calum's mind, and why he had suggested her inclusion on the trip. It just didn't make sense, whichever way you looked at it.

Calum and Alison left soon after that, and Rissa went out to attend to her party of Dutchmen. They all spoke good English and she stayed with them for some time, enjoying their banter and showing them places to visit on the map they had spread out on the table. Finally, they went on their way, having bought several cakes to take with them—this was fast becoming a profitable sideline—and Rissa went back to the kitchen.

'Well, they brightened you up,' Mandy greeted her. 'And I see you've sold half the stock again! You'd better get back to the cooking this afternoon and I'll get Fiona to stay on. She's always glad of an extra few hours. And there's the Edinburgh trip to prepare for, too.'

'Yes. Mandy, why ever did you have to take Calum's side in that? Couldn't you see I didn't want to go? And Alison certainly doesn't want me tagging along. She thought she was going to have Calum all to herself.'

'Exactly.' Mandy looked gravely at her. 'Rissa, I wasn't going to say anything, but—well, I realised the other night just how wrong I'd been, about you and Calum. I thought you didn't like him—thought you loathed him, in fact, and that was why you were always quarrelling. And then, when he came here to dinner and you were so on edge—well, it dawned on me what the trouble really was. You're in love with him, aren't you?'

Rissa sighed. 'Yes, I suppose so. I just wish I weren't. It isn't a pleasant feeling, Mandy.'

'Well, I don't understand that. With me and Donald it's a fantastic feeling—but then we've always understood each other. I think you and Calum have got at cross-purposes and you need to straighten things out. That's why I want you to go to Edinburgh.'

'But it's hopeless, Mandy, can't you see? He doesn't

feel the same way about me—oh, he's attracted to me, he admits that, but it's not love. And nothing else will do for me.' Rissa spoke the last words in a small voice and turned away, while Mandy watched her with compassion.

'Rissa, I'm really sorry. But are you sure that's true? I've seen the way he looks at you sometimes—the way he watches you when you don't know—the way he looks *for* you when he comes here.'

'Yes, I'm absolutely sure. He's told me. Chemistry, that's the word he uses. A kind of fever—a disease. And according to him there's only one cure.' Rissa's eyes filled with tears. 'I can't cure myself that way. For me, it would only make things worse.'

Mandy was silent for a moment. Then she said decisively: 'Well, I don't believe it. I think he does care about you, even if he's not admitting it. I tell you, Rissa, I've seen it in his eyes.'

'And Alison?' Rissa asked dully.

'Oh, she's nothing—she's just on the spot and out to flatter him. You can't blame him for enjoying it, but I bet it won't last. Look, Rissa——' Mandy leaned across the table, her eyes and voice serious '—go to Edinburgh and fight for him. Fight Alison. Because *she'll* fight *you*, whether or not you join in! And I've got a feeling she won't be too choosy with her weapons. But if you want Calum, you've got to do something about it—or you may never get the chance again.'

Rissa stared at her. Was this really Mandy talking, her baby sister who had only just left school, who had never had a serious romance—not counting Donald— and was still more at home in a T-shirt and jeans, pottering about in a boat, than in a smart dress making polite conversation? What did she know about it anyway? But she had to admit that there could be sense in what Mandy said. Could this really be why Calum wanted her along—to see if she *would* fight for him? Did he really have some feeling for her after all?

And if she did fight—and won—what then?

They drove to Edinburgh across the bleak, lonely moors and through the mountain passes to Stirling. It was a chilly, lowering day with the grey clouds pressing down on them just as Rissa's spirits pressed down on her. She sighed and pulled her woollen jacket closer around her, though it wasn't cold in the car. Alison, sitting in front with Calum, had complained about the weather, but she was as elegant as ever in a misty blue tweed suit that nevertheless managed to look totally American. Rissa, in dark brown skirt and cream blouse, felt drab and colourless beside her, and she wondered what it was about Alison that made her own perfectly nice clothes look so nondescript.

She was crazy to have come, crazy to have let Mandy persuade her. She had even allowed them to talk her into staying for two nights instead of the one she had stipulated. Oh, what a fool she was! She felt like asking Calum to turn round now and take her home before they had gone too far, but she knew she wouldn't. And she couldn't stand seeing the gloating triumph that would certainly shine from Alison's cornflower-blue eyes if she did.

They had lunch in Stirling and arrived in Edinburgh just after three o'clock. Alison looked out of the window eagerly, exclaiming with enthusiasm over the beautiful little city. Rissa loved Edinburgh too, but today she couldn't raise any interest. She just wanted the whole trip to be over.

'Oh, it's just perfect!' Alison cried. 'Just look at that delicious little mountain, right in the middle of town! And the castle on top of it—why, that's straight out of fairyland! You've just got to take me up there, Calum. But it's all so *grey*. And the buildings—they don't look English at all.'

'Well, they're not—they're Scottish,' Calum pointed out. 'But a lot of people feel the same when they see them. They do have a foreign look.' He drove into the courtyard of a hotel and stopped. 'This is where we're staying, and I suggest we get ourselves settled in and

then have a look round. I'm afraid the two of you will
have to explore without me tomorrow—I have to see
some people then. Let's have your luggage out.'

The two girls took their cases from the boot—
Alison's of elegant pale blue leather, Rissa's plain,
brown and rather shabby, dating from her college days.
Calum tested their weight, then tucked Rissa's under
one arm and carried his own and Alison's in his hands.
He led the way into the hotel, confirmed their bookings
and handed the girls their keys.

'There's a lift handy,' he remarked, and they travelled
up in silence. Rissa looked at her key, and wondered if
Alison had been disappointed that Calum had booked
separate rooms. But he could hardly have done
otherwise, he was well known in the city. He hadn't
done it because of her presence, she was sure. Calum
wouldn't consider her feelings in *that* respect!

'Here we are,' he said, stopping at one of the doors in
the long corridor. 'Number twenty-six—that's you, isn't
it, Alison?'

'Mm, that's right.' Alison opened the door and gave
a little cry of pleasure. 'What a sweet little room! It's
just ducky, Calum.'

'Good.' He turned to Rissa. 'And we're a little
further along, I think.'

Rissa followed him, aware of Alison's eyes on her
back. Why had he arranged that *she* should be nearer to
him? She stopped at the right door and unlocked it;
then realised with dismay that Calum was unlocking the
next door along.

'Calum!' she whispered, agonised. 'You haven't
booked us next-door rooms?'

'Looks like it,' he said cheerfully. 'What's the
trouble?'

'What's the trouble? What about Alison—she's miles
away!'

'Hardly miles,' he corrected her. 'Yards, yes. I doubt
if she'll faint from lack of nourishment on her way
here—should she need to come here anyway. What are

you worried about, Rissa? She did express pleasure in
her room.'

'Yes, I know, but——' Rissa felt helpless. Calum
knew very well what was in her mind and was just
playing with her. She felt angry. For two pins she would
have gone back to Alison and suggested a swap—but
Mandy's words prevented her. *That* wouldn't be
fighting! And she had promised she *would* fight, though
what for she hardly knew.

Shrugging, she went into her room, Calum following
her with her case, which he set down by the bed. Rissa
looked around. The room was in fact a double one,
with a large bed—had he done that deliberately, too?
she wondered—and a wide window looking out
towards the castle. It was pleasantly furnished and
decorated, in the way of many Scottish hotels—the
emphasis laid on comfort rather than style, the décor
old-fashioned but welcoming.

'All right?' Calum asked, and she nodded.

'It's fine, but I still——'

'So this is where you two are!'

Alison came in, her face sharp with suspicion. She
gave a quick look round the room and Rissa saw her
eyes narrow as they lit on the double bed. 'I thought I'd
just slip along and see that you were both okay. Is this
your room, Calum, or Rissa's?'

'It's mine,' Rissa said quickly. 'Calum just brought
my case in for me.'

'I see.' Again, a quick glance at the bed. 'And where
are you, Cal darling? I was hoping you'd be nearer to
me—just in case I had bad dreams, you know!' A
throaty laugh. 'Let's see your room now, can't we?'

Calum shrugged and led the way out to the next
door. Again Alison's eyes sharpened, but she said
nothing. She followed Calum in and Rissa went last,
feeling forgotten again but this time relieved. The
situation was getting altogether too complicated for her.

'Real cosy, isn't it?' Alison drawled. 'Just like yours,
in fact, Rissa. But—say, tell me if you don't like the

idea, but seeing that I'm a visitor and probably won't ever come to Edinburgh again, would you mind changing rooms with me? I don't have that wonderful view, you see, and I'd just love to be able to wake up in the morning and look out at that fairytale castle up there. What do you say, Rissa? It doesn't really matter to you, does it?'

'Well, I——' Rissa glanced helplessly at Calum, who watched her without expression. Alison laid a hand on her arm and gazed at her beseechingly, and Rissa curbed an impulse to move away. Fight, Mandy had said, but how could you fight this? It would be like boxing with a marshmallow. Oh, what did it matter anyway? Let Alison have what she wanted—she'd make sure she got it one way or another! And at least it would show Calum that Rissa *didn't* always get things her own way—and show him that he wasn't quite so important to her as he obviously believed.

'Yes, of course,' she said. 'I don't mind a bit. Give me your key and I'll take my case along now.'

'You will? Oh, Rissa, you're a real sweetie!' To Rissa's embarrassment, her stepsister kissed her gratefully. 'Isn't she, Cal darling? Isn't she just the sweetest person you've ever known?'

'And just what am I supposed to answer to that?' he asked, with heavy humour. 'It comes into the category of "have you stopped beating your wife" questions. Probably better to say nothing at all.' He turned and unzipped his own suitcase. 'Well, if you two girls want any tea I suggest you sort yourselves out fairly quickly and we meet down in the lounge in about half an hour. They do a very good tea here, or we can go out, whichever you prefer.'

'I'll just do whatever you say, Cal darling,' Alison cooed, and Rissa took her case and went off back down the corridor. She noticed that Alison had brought her case up with her, obviously intending to get Rissa to change rooms whatever the room itself was like—the view had been just an excuse. Fight that, she thought bitterly as she fitted the key in the door of number twenty-six. The only way to fight Alison was by using her own weapons of cunning and sheer ruthlessness. And that was something Rissa just wasn't prepared to do.

Tea was in a grand style, served in a lounge full of Scotswomen, evidently in the city for a day's shopping, and a clutch of American tourists. Rissa, Calum and Alison sat back in deep armchairs and helped themselves to tiny sandwiches, buttered scones and chocolate eclairs. The tea was brown and strong, reviving flagging spirits, and even Rissa felt better after it. She sipped slowly, keeping out of the conversation, and again wondered why Calum had asked her to come. To keep Alison company tomorrow, perhaps? But he must have realised that either girl would rather be alone. And she felt sad at the thought; once upon a time she and Alison had been friends. Or so she had thought—but that was in the days when she had hero-worshipped Alison for her poise and beauty. Now she saw those things as a mere façade, and hadn't yet discovered anything underneath the polish. Was there anything—something that Calum had discovered, perhaps? Or was she right to suspect that Alison was not much more than a beautiful shell?

'Now I want you to show me Edinburgh,' Alison announced, throwing down her napkin. 'Starting with the Castle. Or is it too late to see that now?'

'Probably. You'd better leave that till tomorrow, when you've more time. I'll take you for a walk round the streets, though. You ought to see Princes Street, of course, and the Royal Mile—and there are a hundred tiny cobbled back streets which are absolutely fascinating. I can see Rissa poking about amongst them for hours!' He smiled at Rissa, including her in the conversation for the first time, but Alison wrinkled her nose.

'Poking about amongst back streets—ugh! That

wasn't what I came to Edinburgh for. Though I can imagine Rissa enjoying it.' Her words only just stopped short of hinting that Rissa would actually feel at home there. She helped herself to a piece of shortbread. 'You know, I just can't resist these gorgeous cookies. What my agent's going to say about my figure when I get back home, I just don't know!'

'Well, it looks all right to me,' Calum murmured with a suggestive glance, and Alison gurgled with laughter.

'Trust you to take me up on *that*! Well, maybe I won't worry then. So long as *you* appreciate me—could be it won't matter too much what my agent thinks, hmm?'

Rissa turned away. Was she really expected to sit here and listen to this? she wondered. She glanced at Calum and found him watching her, an odd expression on his face. Perhaps she could get out of whatever he had planned for the rest of the day—feign a headache, or something.

But Calum wasn't having that. Her faint protests were met with the equable remark that fresh air was what she needed after the long drive, and he kept his hand firmly under her arm as if to prevent her escaping as they left the hotel. And it did seem to be better outside. With more space around them she was less conscious of Alison's presence, and after a while she managed to drop back behind them in the narrow street, pretending an interest she didn't really feel in the tiny shop windows.

'You're right, Calum, these streets are real quaint,' Alison conceded as he led them through the maze of cobbled streets and alleys. 'But I do want to see Princes Street and the Royal Mile too—I've heard so much about them. Can't we go there too?'

'Certainly. You can cut through here, look. But you won't be able to do much shopping now, Alison, they're just on the point of closing.'

'We'll window-shop, then.' She tucked her hand

through his arm and smiled up at him. 'I can make plans for tomorrow.'

They drifted slowly along Princes Street, looking in the windows at the goods arrayed there. Alison exclaimed with pleasure at the Scottish tweeds and plaids, the knitwear and the glass and jewellery. It looked as if they were in for a busy time tomorrow, Rissa thought, wondering if they would ever get as far as visiting the castle. Somehow, she thought not; Alison was clearly a city girl, uninterested in the historical or architectural beauties that struck Rissa at every turn. She might make a display of interest to impress Calum, but left to herself the shops would take up all her time.

At last the American girl admitted that her feet were hurting her and she'd just love to sit down for a while. Calum suggested returning to the hotel. 'You can rest properly there,' he said, 'and we'll go out to dinner later on.'

'Dinner in Edinburgh,' Alison sighed. 'It's all just too romantic!' A tiny pause, then she added just a shade too casually: 'How about you, Rissa? Want to come along, or is that head of yours still bad?'

'Oh, Rissa will come too,' Calum said quickly, before Rissa could speak. 'I know those headaches of hers, they never last long, do they, Rissa?'

Rissa glared at him. She rarely had headaches and had never, to her knowledge, had one while Calum was around. Clearly he didn't believe in this one. But his hard, bright gaze told her that any protest would be firmly overruled, and she couldn't face any more arguments. She shrugged and muttered that she would probably be all right, and in fact did feel better in the fresh air.

'Well, that's just fine,' said Alison in a tone that said the opposite. 'But you mustn't be afraid to say if you change your mind, Rissa. And maybe an early night would be a good idea, hmm?'

'You're being very solicitous, Alison,' Calum remarked. 'Rissa's very lucky to have such a caring stepsister to look after her. Must make quite a change for you, eh, Rissa?'

This had both girls glancing at him suspiciously, but there was nothing to learn from his expression, and nothing more was said until they returned to the hotel.

They reached Rissa's room first and she went in, arranging to meet again later to go out to dinner. Alison, looking smug, went on along the corridor with Calum, and Rissa shut her door quickly; she didn't want to see if they both went into the same room. But thoughts of what might be happening tormented her as she went over to her window and opened it to lean out.

That headache could easily become a reality. She could already feel a dull heaviness over her eyes. Perhaps a bath or shower would be a good idea—and then a rest until it was time to go out again. Moving slowly, she gathered up her things and slipped out to the bathroom.

The hotel was as old-fashioned in its plumbing as in everything else, and even in her dulled state of mind Rissa couldn't help being amused by the bathroom. What would Alison make of it, she wondered, with its huge bath and great taps that must have been easily a foot long. The water that gushed from them was certainly hot, though, and she lay back in it, letting its warmth soak into her tired limbs and relax the tautness of her body. Here, at least, she was safe; nobody could get at her. And she almost wished that she could stay there until the entire visit was over.

But she had to get out in the end, and she dried herself and wrapped a bathrobe round her before going back to her room. Carrying her soap, sponge and towel, she padded along the corridor, wondering what the time was and if it was too late to have that doze on her bed.

Reaching her door, she frowned. Surely she couldn't have left it unlocked? But it was ajar now, so she must have. Had anyone been in while she was away? Well, they would have been disappointed if they were looking for valuables, she reflected grimly as she pushed it fully open. Alison was the one whose room they ought to have gone into for that, and she——

'Calum!'

He was lying back on her bed, his shoes off, arms behind his head. He had changed for the evening, she noticed, but his jacket hung over a chair and he looked casual and relaxed in an ice-grey shirt that matched his steely eyes. There was a twinkle in those eyes now as they looked out at her from under the shaggy brows, and she closed the door quickly and stood against it, her heart thundering under the thin robe.

'Calum, what are you doing here? How did you get in?'

'Easily enough. I asked at the desk for a spare key—told them you wanted me to take something in and had gone into the bathroom without leaving it open. They know me here, there was no problem.'

'Perhaps they're used to you having the key to women's rooms,' Rissa flashed, but it didn't have the effect on him that she'd hoped. Instead of getting angry, he just laughed and said: 'Perhaps. Or perhaps they think I'm completely trustworthy.'

'In which case, they *don't* know you!'

'Well, we won't argue about that. Anyway, it's a purely friendly visit. I just wanted to know how your head is.'

Rissa glared at him. 'You never believed there was anything wrong with it.'

'Didn't I? Then perhaps you can tell me what *you* think the reason is for this visit.'

'Oh, you're impossible!' Rissa turned away and put her washing things down on the dressing-table. 'Look, I want to get dressed. Will you please go away?'

'Why? I've seen you dress before.' His eyes moved over her. 'And very nice it was too.'

'Oh, for heaven's sake! What are you trying to do—drive me insane? Calum, I never wanted to come on this trip and I'm certain that Alison didn't want me along. I don't even begin to understand why you asked me——

more or less *forced* me. And I can see I'm nothing more than a spare part now I'm here. So why don't you just leave me alone—take Alison out to dinner, it's what she wants and what you want too. Why keep dragging me into it?'

'Why not?' With a single movement, he was on his feet and his hands were feeling her body through the thin material of her bathrobe. He pulled her close and laid one hand over her heart. 'Don't tell me this isn't doing something to you, Rissa,' he murmured, his voice deep in her ear. 'Your heart's going like a steam-hammer. And if you want an answer to at least one of those questions—yes, I do want to drive you insane. Like this. . . .'

He slipped his hand into the open neck of her robe, pulling it away to expose her rounded breasts, still rosy from the bath. His fingers caressed her lightly; then, lifting the curve towards his lips, he kissed it. His other hand supported her back and instinctively she let her body take the arch that brought her into even closer contact with him. A surge of hot desire raced through her body and she knew that her feelings for Calum hadn't lessened since the last time he had touched her; they had intensified. There was no way she could resist him now, no way at all, and almost without her willing it, her arms went up round his neck, pulling him even closer as her fingers tangled in the thick black hair.

With a muttered exclamation, Calum lifted her in his arms and held her against him before laying her on the bed. She looked up at his face, feeling the glow that spread through her, knowing that her desire and love must be shining from her eyes. And in his eyes she saw an answering emotion. Desire, yes—and love? Could it be love? Was Mandy right after all—and was *this* why he had brought her to Edinburgh?

'Calum——' she whispered, but he shook his head and laid his fingers over her lips.

'Don't talk. Don't say anything. There's only one way to communicate, and it's worth a thousand speeches. I can tell you all you need to know with my body, Rissa—just as you can tell me everything with yours. Forget your tongue can talk and let it find another way to speak to me.' He covered her mouth with his own and ran his tongue gently round her parted lips, and she moaned with pleasure. 'Talk to me like this, Rissa,' he murmured, finding her hand and drawing it down to his body. 'This way, there can be no misunderstanding.'

Rissa closed her eyes and gave herself up to the delicious sensations that were now taking over, making her body move in a way she had never dreamed of, forcing her mind to take second place as an instinct older than thought took complete control. The bathrobe fell away from her body and Calum began a series of kisses that left her burning from head to toe. She twisted herself in his arms, wanting to come even closer; twined her legs around his and longed to feel his skin against hers. Already she had unbuttoned his shirt, although she had no memory of it, and the rough hairiness of his broad chest pressed against her soft breasts, making her gasp with the delight of the contact. She trailed her fingers through the curling black hairs, down to his waist, and fumbled with the fastening there; and then froze with horror as she heard a knock on the door.

'Rissa!' Alison's voice called, high and sweet. 'Are you there, honey? I want to borrow a clothes-brush if you have one.'

Rissa stared at Calum in panic and he closed his eyes, then jerked his head towards the door. Alison was already knocking again when Rissa scrambled off the bed, dragging the robe round her, and ran to the door. She opened it, wondering just how long she could hold Alison at bay, wondering too if her flushed face and quick breathing was going to give her away.

Alison was wearing a bathrobe too, only hers wasn't an ordinary chain-store one like Rissa's; hers was an ethereal, floating affair of pale green chiffon that made her look like a mermaid with her pale hair streaming down to her shoulders. She gave Rissa a wide smile that did nothing to hide the hard suspicion in her eyes and said sweetly: 'Sorry to bother you, hon, but I seem to have forgotten my clothes-brush and I can't seem to find Calum. I suppose he's in his bath—oh! *There* you are, Cal darling. What a surprise!'

She pushed past Rissa and glanced sharply around, taking in everything. Rissa saw to her relief that Calum had managed to pull the bedspread flat and was now standing by the window, his shirt buttoned and tucked in. He must have moved fast—though why he shouldn't come along and make love to Rissa if he wanted to, she didn't really know, she thought with a jolt of surprise. He wasn't *married* to Alison, after all! All the same, she was aware of relief that there was nothing Alison could really object to in the situation. She didn't want any scenes now, not until she had got her relationship with Calum really sorted out.

'Well, isn't that a coincidence,' Calum was saying lazily, returning Alison's stare with a look of bland innocence. 'I just came along to borrow a brush too. Aren't we lucky that Rissa packed so well? You do have one, I suppose?'

'Oh—yes.' Glad to be able to turn away from that suspicious stare of Alison's, Rissa rummaged in her bag and produced the brush. Not that it was much of an excuse, she thought; Alison was the last person to forget such an important item, and Calum probably next to last. But he had neatly hoisted the American girl with her own petard; having used the excuse herself first, she could hardly accuse him of having made it up.

'I'll bring it back in a few minutes,' Calum promised as they went out, a gleam in his eye. But Alison, evidently still unsure of what had actually been going on but determined not to let it happen again, said quickly: 'Oh no, Calum. You're dressed—*you* have it first, and I'll bring it back. In fact——' she added with a glance of pure malice at Rissa as they went out through

the door '—since you've already got your trousers on
I'll come in and brush you down. It'll save you taking
them off again, won't it!'

Round to Alison there, Rissa thought. But as she closed
the door and leaned back against it, she couldn't help
a wave of pure happiness washing over her. The
interruption didn't really matter at all. She was surer
now of Calum's feelings than she had ever been. Sure
enough now to take Mandy's advice and fight for him.

But there was, after all, no chance to fight that evening.
They had scarcely sat down in the restaurant Calum
had taken them to when he was hailed by a man already
in there, sitting alone at a small table. He hadn't started
his own meal yet, and with a quick word to the waiter
he hurried over.

'Calum! This is a lucky chance—I was going to get
hold of you in the next day or two. Look, I want a
word about rehearsals——' He broke off, noticing the
two girls. 'Heck, I'm sorry, I didn't realise you were
together. I'd better get back to my table. Maybe we can
fix something for tomorrow.'

'No, I'm tied up all tomorrow.' Calum turned to the
girls. 'Sorry, but if Victor says he needs to talk to me
it's probably important—he's my conductor in the
Festival performance. Do you mind if he shares our
table?'

'Of course not,' Rissa said at once. Alison looked put
out, but merely shrugged and said: 'If it's that
important. . . .' Calum turned back to Victor, a dapper
little man who must, Rissa realised, be Victor Morris,
the famous conductor. She looked at him with interest;
she had listened to many concerts he had conducted
and had several records of his as well. It would be
fascinating to share a meal with him and listen to him
and Calum talking shop—an opportunity, too, to see
that vital side of Calum which was his professional life.
And it would postpone the conflict with Alison that she
knew now would have to come.

In fact, much of the talk went over her head, but she was fascinated all the same—unlike Alison who, after half an hour, made no attempt to hide her boredom and occupied herself by looking critically at the other diners and commenting on their dress and appearance. Rissa tried to ignore her; she didn't want Calum to think that this was *her* main interest too. But after one or two glances she realised that he wanted her to keep Alison quiet, so reluctantly she abandoned her attempts to understand their conversation and gave Alison her attention instead.

She was relieved when the meal was over, but even then it seemed that Calum and Victor still had a lot to discuss, and she was forced to agree when Calum suggested that she and Alison should return to the hotel while he went back to Victor's lodgings to work out some difficulties in the score for the concerto. Again, she could see that Alison was no better pleased, but it seemed that there was little choice. And at least when they got back she could shut herself into her room, alone.

She had scarcely done so when there was a knock on the door and Alison appeared.

'Hullo, Alison. Did you want something?' Rissa kept her voice light but eyed the other girl warily. This was no social call, she'd be willing to bet, and Alison's next words confirmed this.

'I suppose you think you're being very clever!'

'I don't know what you mean.'

The American girl snorted derisively. 'Like hell you don't! I wouldn't put it past you to have *arranged* for that Victor guy to run into us in that restaurant——'

'Don't be ridiculous! I've never even met him—he's a famous conductor.'

'And Calum's a famous pianist. That's his attraction for you, isn't it? That, and the fact that he's rich and all man.'

'You're talking nonsense,' Rissa said coldy. 'And if you don't mind, I think I'll have that early night you were talking about earlier.'

'Hoping lover-boy will call in later, are you?' Alison sneered. 'Oh, you don't have to look so innocent—*I* know what was going on in here this afternoon. Or what you *hoped* would go on. But let me save you any further trouble, honey-child. Cal might just take a slice or two of what you're offering him, he wouldn't be a man if he didn't, but that particular cake is mine, get it? When this Festival is over, Cal and I are going to get married, and nothing that happens between him and you or any other girl in the meantime is going to make one ounce of difference!'

Rissa turned her back, hoping that Alison wouldn't see how her body was shaking. 'I don't believe you!'

'No? Well, you'll just have to wait and see, won't you? But my advice to you is, steer well clear of Cal in the next few weeks, unless you're a lot tougher than I think you are. He may not be out to hurt you, but that's how it'll end up. He's going to make the most of his last few weeks of freedom, isn't he, and any girl who hands it to him on a plate the way you are is going to get all she asks for. Don't say you haven't been warned!'

'And you'd put up with that? You'd agree to marry him, knowing that he was going to be unfaithful to you?' Rissa didn't even try to keep the disbelief out of her voice, and Alison laughed.

'You just can't understand it, can you, prim little English miss! But then you've always led a pretty sheltered life, haven't you? That's what makes you such easy game. Look——' she moved closer and Rissa could see the feverish glitter in her eyes '——Cal and I have both been around. We know the game inside out and backwards. Cal won't be unfaithful to me—not after we're married. You can bet on that. But up till then—well, he's his own man, and I won't blame him if he feels like a last fling or two. It'll make it easier for him to settle down afterwards.' She smiled a catlike smile. 'I'm not warning you off, Rissa. I'm just telling you for your own good. Cal's a compulsive womaniser, didn't you know that?'

'No, I didn't, and I don't know it now.' Rissa's voice shook. 'I've known Calum all my life and I don't think he's like that. All right, he's had girl-friends, but he's over thirty, so what does that mean? And he's said nothing to me about marrying you.'

'I should hope not, since we agreed to keep it a secret till after the Festival.' Alison's flowerlike eyes assessed her coldly. 'I just wonder what it'll take to make you believe me? Maybe if you heard a few things you *didn't* know about Cal—like some of the particular "girl-friends" he's had!'

'What do you mean?' Rissa had gone cold. She stared at Alison, wondering what lay behind those beautiful eyes, wondering where all the spite and malice had come from. Had they always been there, or was it something that had happened recently? And why should she vent them on Rissa? Suddenly she knew that she didn't want to hear what Alison was going to say, and she turned away again.

'Don't say any more,' she begged. 'Just go away. Calum will choose whichever one of us he wants, if he wants us at all, and I'll go along with his choice if you will.'

'Oh no!' Alison's voice was like fine silk. 'I don't let fate run my life. I take a hand in it myself. And this is something I think you ought to know.' She paused. 'You don't believe me when I say that Calum's a compulsive womaniser, do you? You don't believe that he's only interested in one thing apart from his music— sex. But he's a highly sensitive creative artist, Rissa, and he has to stoke himself up somehow. And sex is the best way—look at any artist. Plenty of them have the same reputation.'

'And that's virtually slander,' retorted Rissa, but Alison shook her head.

'Sex and creativity go together, and Calum's never been one to deny himself.' She paused. 'Even when he was quite young. At that age an older woman can be very attractive. And there aren't all that many women around at Ichrachan.'

Rissa turned and stared at her. What was she saying? She cast her mind round wildly, trying to fathom out a meaning; then, slowly, she remembered Calum as a boy, a slim, dark teenager with a haunted face and tormented eyes, coming to Cluny Cottage to talk to her mother, the only person who understood him. Spending long hours alone with her. . . .

'*No!*' she cried, the colour leaving her cheeks so quickly that she felt sick and giddy. 'No—it's not true, it's a filthy, disgusting lie—I don't believe it, I *won't*!'

'Why not?' Alison asked coolly. 'He was old enough—he was twenty-one when she died, wasn't he? What's so disgusting and filthy about that? Just because she was your mother?' She paused again, looking away from Rissa, then swung her glance back. 'It was the same with my mother too.'

'With *Kate*?' The words were a whisper now.

'Yes. Why else do you think Cal and I broke up? I found out—and, like you, I was pretty cut up about it. Thank God I'm older now and a bit more realistic.'

This time Rissa was forced to sit down. She stared at Alison, her eyes wide and horrified. Was it really true? Wasn't it just a vicious lie?

'Ask him, if you like,' Alison said calmly. 'It might even help him to make that choice you were talking about. He knows *I'm* never going to throw it in his face.'

But Rissa knew that she could never face Calum with that question. And she knew that it was the end of any relationship between them, because in such a relationship she had to have truth. She could never live with Calum, knowing that perhaps once he had made love to both Kate and her mother. All right, to the modern viewpoint it shouldn't really matter—but to Rissa it did. And to ask him would have betrayed the trust that must, if they were to make any kind of life together, stand firm between them.

'All right, Alison,' she said dully. 'You've won. You can leave me alone now—I'll be going home first thing tomorrow.'

Alison looked at her for a long moment, then apparently decided that Rissa meant what she said. A look of unmistakable triumph came into her eyes. She nodded complacently.

'You're a good loser, Rissa,' she offered. A better one than I am—but I never had any intention of losing. Can I give you just one more piece of advice? Get away before Calum sees you in the morning—it'll be easier all round.'

'Just go away,' Rissa said flatly. 'Just leave me alone.'

The American girl shrugged. 'Suits me, honey. I was only trying to help.' She turned to the door. 'See you around, kid. Maybe I'll even send you an invitation to the wedding—or would that be too much like gloating?' She opened the door and jumped. 'Hey, I didn't know there was anyone out there. You gave me quite a fright!' A small pause, and then she said in a different tone: 'Say, aren't you *Alistair*? The one who went to be a doctor? What——'

But she got no further. Rissa had sat up as if electrified at the name. She jumped to her feet, feeling a great surge of relief, and ran across the room, pushing Alison aside. Alistair! It was really Alistair, standing there with a grin of surprise on his pleasant face, Alistair looking solid and dependable, Alistair who would take over from here, look after her and make everything right again.

'Oh, *Alistair!*' she cried, and flung herself into his arms, weeping as if her heart would break.

CHAPTER EIGHT

ALISTAIR held her in his arms, one hand patting her shaking shoulders, the other gently stroking her hair. Rissa clung to him, pouring all her grief and bewilderment out in her tears. How or why he had arrived at just that moment, she had no idea. It was enough that he was there.

'A touching little scene,' Alison remarked. 'I take it you two mean something to each other? What a lucky chance, you turning up just now, Alistair.'

Rissa raised her head. Alison's insinuating voice angered her, but somehow the other girl didn't matter quite so much now. 'How *did* you know I was here, Alistair?' she asked wonderingly. 'I thought you were in Glasgow.'

'Well, I was. But I've come over to Edinburgh to study some new treatment methods they've got here. It's a subject I'm rather interested in—I'd been thinking of specialising—so I've been offered a course. It came up at pretty short notice or I'd have let you know—but when I rang Cluny Cottage and Mandy told me you were here I just had to take the opportunity of seeing you.' He glanced down at Rissa's tear-stained face. 'It looks as if I arrived at the right moment, too. What's been going on?'

'Oh—I can't explain.' It was too complicated, and she certainly couldn't go into it all with Alison standing there with that smug expression on her face. 'Alistair, I want to go home. There's no place for me here. I should never have come.'

'Would you like me to take you?' he asked, quietly, and she nodded, her eyes brimming again.

'Oh, Alistair, if only you could! But surely you have to be at the hospital all day? How——'

'If it's that bad,' he told her, 'I'll take you now. I could be back for the morning and I'm used to missing my sleep.'

'I couldn't ask you to do that!' Rissa exclaimed, but the thought of getting away from here now, away from Alison's complacency and Calum's conceit, was too much for her, and Alistair read the longing in her face.

'You don't have to ask. I told you, if ever you needed me I was your man.' He touched her cheek with his finger. 'Can you pack your things, Rissa, or shall I help you?'

'Such a little gentleman!' Alison sneered. 'Yes, you help her, Alistair. She's right—there is no place for her here. It's a pity she couldn't have realised it before.'

Alistair turned to her and looked her up and down. Her beauty and femininity seemed to make no impression on him at all; there was no widening of the eyes, no appreciative assessment. His voice was cold as he spoke.

'The person there's no place for in this room is you, Alison. Why don't you go and leave Rissa and me alone? Considering the state Rissa was in when I arrived, it's a pity *you* didn't think to do it a lot sooner.'

'Well!' Alison exclaimed. 'Not such a little gentleman after all! All right, I'm going—I was just about to anyway. And Rissa's more than welcome to you—if you ask me, Ichrachan's got more than its fair share of Scottish yokels!'

She slammed the door, and Rissa curbed a hysterical desire to laugh. But she wasn't really amused and she suspected that if she did laugh she would end up crying. Anyway, there was nothing to wait for now. For the time being, at least, she felt better. The best thing for her to do now would be to get her packing done—that wouldn't take long. And then she could be on her way home—safe, with Alistair at her side.

The journey took several hours and they finally arrived at Cluny Cottage in the early hours of the morning.

Mandy, warned by telephone while Rissa was packing, had gone to bed but left a casserole simmering gently in the Rayburn oven, and both Rissa and Alistair were glad of it, though Rissa could eat only a few mouthfuls. Her first painful distress had dulled and she now felt numb. She wished she could go to sleep, wake tomorrow and find it had all been a bad dream. She wished she had never come back to Cluny in the first place.

Alistair hadn't asked any questions, for which she was grateful, but he deserved an explanation. The trouble was how much to tell him. She couldn't—she just couldn't—tell him of Alison's dreadful accusations about her mother and Kate. Nor could she tell him about the scene in her bedroom just before Alison had come along with the excuse about the clothes-brush. And there wasn't really much else to tell. Helplessly, she fumbled with her words until Alistair, a compassionate smile on his face, reached across the table and covered her hand with his.

'Don't worry, Rissa. I can see it didn't work out, whatever it was, and I've more than a clue as to whose fault it was too. Calum's a bigger fool than I ever thought if he prefers that little hellcat to you. But some men are fools, and maybe you're well out of it. You just get off to bed now, and have a good rest. And then try to put him out of your mind.' He grinned suddenly, looking boyish. 'As your doctor, I'd recommend a nice long holiday in the sun, with medical attention from me! But I don't suppose you'll take my advice—though a break would probably do you the world of good.'

'I know. And once the summer's over I promise I'll take one.' Rissa stood up and yawned, suddenly weary. 'Alistair, I really can't thank you enough for bringing me home. I just wish you didn't have to drive all that way back so late.'

'Don't give it a thought. Like I said, I'm used to being up all night and I haven't been over-stretching myself these past few days.' He stood up too and kissed

her lightly. 'I'm glad I could help, Rissa. Don't forget—
I'm always around, a telephone call away.'

'Thank you, Alistair. And you might use that phone
to let me know you've arrived safely!' She slipped her
arms round his neck and kissed him back. 'You're a
good friend to me—the best I've got.'

'Well, that's something anyway,' he remarked, and
went out of the cottage, whistling. Rissa watched him
drive away; then, slowly, she locked the door, cleared
away their dishes and climbed the stairs.

It seemed a long time since she had left the cottage on
the ill-fated trip to Edinburgh. It would be even longer,
she vowed, before she allowed anyone to persuade her
out of it again.

Rissa did not wake next morning until the sun was high
in the sky. For a few minutes she lay looking in a dazed
fashion out through the window. Why was she still in
bed, so late? Had she been ill? Surely she could hear
customers downstairs, and Fiona's chatty lilting voice.
Bewildered, she put a hand to her forehead—and then
remembered everything.

With a groan, she turned her face into the pillow. She
recalled the spite on Alison's face as she had told her
about Calum's affairs with Rissa's mother and
stepmother—Alison's mother—too. Could it really be
true? But in a grim way, it all fitted. Calum *had* been a
frequent visitor to Cluny Cottage when Rissa was a
child, and had spent many hours with Mrs Loring. And
Kate had been to Cluny before Alison, that time when
Rissa and Mandy had been staying with their
godparents in Devon. A second honeymoon, Kate had
called it, making up for a brief few days they had had
after their marriage just before Christmas. Could
another affair have started then? And continued
through all those years when Rissa hadn't been to
Ichrachan?

It didn't bear thinking about. Not her lovely, gentle
mother, not the stepmother who had been so kind to

her. But Rissa had experienced enough during the past weeks to know that Calum could be a very persuasive lover indeed. She wasn't proof against him herself—did she have any right to suppose that other women were? So far, the signs were all to the opposite.

If only she'd never gone to Edinburgh! If only she had ignored Mandy's advice and allowed Alison to win without a fight. She would never have heard that dreadful revelation then, would never be suffering this misery now.

Well, there was only one cure that she knew. Work. And Rissa, thrusting her unhappiness away with an almost physical effort, pushed herself out of bed and felt in the wardrobe for her working clothes.

That was better. She would at least look like herself now. And perhaps, with time, she would feel like herself too. Only time itself would tell.

Mandy was concerned to see her sister downstairs again, and urged her to go back to bed, or at least rest. But Rissa shook her head and even managed to summon up a smile.

'I'm not ill, Mandy,' she insisted. 'And the best thing for me is something to do. I'll make scones all day if you won't let me do anything else! Edinburgh was a mistake, that's all. I should never have gone.'

'It was my fault,' Mandy said remorsefully, looking at the dark shadows under Rissa's eyes, showing up all the more against her pale face. 'I kept on at you, and I knew you didn't really want to go. But honestly, I thought it would be a good thing. Why should Alison get all her own way, after all?'

'Well, at least you seem to have seen through her too. I was afraid she'd pulled the wool over your eyes too, at first.'

'Oh, that soon rubbed off,' Mandy said lightly. 'She tried to flirt with Donald, you know, and he wasn't having any. I realised then what she was like. What I *didn't* realise at first was that you—well, were fond of Calum. Or I wouldn't have encouraged her there.'

'Well, you don't need to worry any more. Any chance there might have been for Calum and me has finally and definitely gone. And I can see more customers coming. Am I to be allowed to serve them, or are you in charge here now?' She paused in the doorway and said gently, 'Don't blame yourself, Mandy. We do all have to work out our own lives, don't we? And I'll tell you about it later on.'

She didn't tell Mandy everything, but she did give her a brief résumé of the events in Edinburgh, keeping back Alison's final revelation concerning their own mother. That was something she couldn't repeat. She did ask, tentatively, about Kate's visits to Cluny, and Mandy wrinkled her brow.

'Yes, we did see a fair amount of Calum when he was at Kilvanie,' she admitted. 'Oh, but surely there was nothing like that between him and Kate, Rissa. She loved Dad—she wouldn't have treated him like that. How could Alison make such an accusation about her own mother? What kind of a person would that make her?'

'The kind of person I suspect she is. Oh, I don't know, Mandy. Let's leave it. We'll never know the truth anyway—and as I doubt very much if we'll see a lot of any of them in the future, maybe it's not worth worrying about.' She knew, even as she spoke, that those wise words wouldn't stop *her* from worrying about it, but she didn't like to see that bewildered look on Mandy's face. 'Look, there's something else I wanted to say.' She paused. 'About you and Donald—I was wrong there, Mandy. You were right—I can't run my own life properly and I've no right at all to try to run yours. You're eighteen, old enough to make up your own mind, and I won't interfere any more. If you want to stay here and marry Donald, you go ahead and do it. I'll wish you every happiness.'

Mandy raised her head, and Rissa swallowed as she saw the radiance sweep into the vivid face. Joyfully, her young sister jumped up and embraced her, half

laughing and half crying; while Rissa held her,
astonished that she could have caused such jubilation
and wondering remorsefully if she had caused an equal
amount of misery through her disapproval.

'It really *will* be all right,' Mandy assured her. 'We'd
worked it all out—I can go on helping you here, and
Donald will work in the hotel, and we'll save like mad
for the new boat. He wants to use it partly for tourists,
partly for fishing. People could charter it. In fact, he's
been thinking of getting a ketch or something like that
and taking people on sailing holidays. I'd go too, of
course. It would cost a lot, but you can get mortgages
for boats and——' She chattered on, all the plans she
and Donald had made spilling out, while Rissa listened
bemused. They really had worked out all the details, she
thought. Much more than she ever had, drifting vaguely
from school to college, from college to job, from job up
here to Cluny. If Mandy had the brains, she was
certainly using them, and for the first time Rissa saw
their future in their terms rather than the bleak prospect
she had seen before.

'Ask Donald to supper tomorrow,' she suggested.
'We'll have a celebration.'

'In the tea-room, with candles?' asked Mandy with a
wicked look.

'If you like,' said Rissa, and Mandy laughed and
shook her head.

'We'll be happy with a pot-luck meal round the
kitchen table. That's the kind of life we like—and you
don't want to be giving us grand ideas!'

Rissa remembered her idea about serving evening
meals. Maybe it would be a good thing to ex-
pand—but she had a suspicion she wouldn't be
keeping Mandy for long. Let Donald get that ketch
and the two of them would be living aboard it, taking
advantage of every excuse to put to sea. They were
like two children—but two happy children, who had
their priorities right and their heads screwed on.
Nothing very terrible would go wrong for Mandy and

Donald, as long as they loved each other as they did now.

Rissa stifled a sigh and got up. It was still early, dusk only just falling over the loch, but she was aware of a tiredness that had come from more than today's work.

'I think I'll go to bed now,' she said. 'You go and see Donald, and plan when this wedding's going to take place. And then I suppose I'd better think about making a wedding-cake.' She smiled. 'Don't make it too soon; the cake will need at least two months to mature.'

'Then perhaps we'd better just have scones and rock buns,' Mandy laughed. 'Because now that we know you're happy about it, there's nothing else to wait for.'

Her words touched Rissa deeply. After all her objections, Mandy had still wanted to wait. She hadn't gone ahead with her plans in spite of her sister, as she so easily could have done. She had wanted Rissa to be happy about it; it had mattered to her. Now, happiness shone from her like warmth from the sun, and Rissa realised for the first time the responsibility that came with running other people's lives, even when, as children, they needed the guidance. And the greatest part of that responsibility was in knowing when to let go.

I've made a mess of most things so far, she thought, watching her sister flit amongst the tables in the garden. Mandy's a wiser person than I am, even if she is five years younger.

She wondered what would happen when Calum and Alison returned tomorrow. Well, at least Alison had got what she wanted, Calum to herself in Edinburgh. She would probably spend today shopping, but tonight they would be together. What delight she must have taken in telling him that Rissa had returned to Cluny. Rissa wondered just what Calum's reaction had been. Anger, certainly. Disappointment—well, perhaps. But Alison would have known how to deal with that. Probably by now he was quite glad that Rissa had gone. He must have realised himself what a mistake it had been for her to accompany them.

Well, when they came back tomorrow perhaps there would be another engagement to celebrate, though there wouldn't be much celebrating going on at Cluny Cottage. Mandy had made it quite clear what her feelings were now towards her stepsister, and Alison surely wouldn't want to continue staying here in those circumstances. More than likely she would simply move into Kilvanie with Calum. The thought gave Rissa a sharp pang.

Rissa spent the day baking, and felt a sense of achievement as she surveyed the fruits of her labours at the end of the day. Scones, flapjacks, fruit cakes, apricot loaves, treacle tarts, Scotch pancakes, fudge squares—they should last for a few days anyway. She liked to get ahead, so that there was always a few days' supply in the bins and the freezer. Especially as, with so many people asking to buy cakes and scones to take away with them, the supply could run short very quickly indeed.

All the same, she was beginning to wonder whether those flashes of despair, that feeling that she should never have returned here, didn't represent her true feelings. *Had* it been such a good idea? Since she'd come back, there had been nothing but pain and unhappiness for her. For Mandy, it had been right; but for her?

Well, and what was there to keep her here, once Mandy was settled? She and Donald could live in Cluny Cottage—they could still run the tea-room if they wanted to, or close it down, whichever they preferred. At present, Rissa did the baking, but Mandy could take that over—her cooking had improved rapidly, she made beautifully light scones, and the other things were easy enough. Help was available from the village too. It would increase the young couple's income, and the two ventures—the tea-room and Donald's boat—would go well together.

Wasn't it the answer? Wouldn't it be better all round

if Rissa went away—left Cluny, left Scotland altogether perhaps, and found another job? Perhaps she could try hotel work, living-in. Or get a housekeeper's post somewhere. Anywhere, so long as she was safe from Calum and the memories that Ichrachan held for her. Anywhere where she could make a fresh start, build a new life.

She would talk to Mandy and Donald about it tonight, at supper.

As she had half expected, they didn't take to the idea with any immediate enthusiasm, though Rissa could see that they appreciated the possibilities. Mandy protested that they didn't want to drive Rissa out of her home, that they'd wanted to go on as they were now, and Donald agreed.

'This is your home, Rissa,' he pointed out. 'Why should you leave it just because Mandy's fool enough to want to marry me?'

'Well, that isn't the whole reason,' Rissa told him, wondering how much he knew of her story. 'And it can still be my home, can't it? I can use the small room to sleep in when I visit you, and keep a few things. You won't be getting rid of me entirely, Donald—I shall keep on turning up like a bad penny!'

'Aye, but it doesn't seem right,' he persisted. 'There's no reason why you *should* go. You like it here, you've only been back five minutes. Why go dashing off again? The tea-room's doing well. I don't understand.'

'I do,' Mandy said quietly. 'As Rissa said, she has her own reasons. And it needn't be for ever, need it? You could come back any time.'

'Yes, of course,' Rissa agreed, but she knew she wouldn't. Once she had left Ichrachan she wouldn't return for more than the odd few days. It could never be her home again.

'But what are you going to do?' Donald's pleasant face was creased with worry. 'You can't go off into the blue without a job, or anything. I don't like it, Rissa, it's all too sudden. Are you sure you're happy about Mandy and me? I should hate to think——'

Rissa smiled at him, suddenly glad to think that he was going to be her brother-in-law. 'You don't have to think anything,' she said. 'I won't go off without making sure I've got something to do to. I thought of a hotel, or perhaps a housekeeper somewhere—a living-in job. I'll still think of this as my home, and you'll probably get heartily sick of me popping up on the doorstep! And as for being happy about you and Mandy—well, I just can't wait to get you safe into the family. I don't know how we've ever managed without you!'

Donald looked appeased but still not completely satisfied. He opened his mouth to speak again; but before he could say anything, the telephone shrilled.

'I'll answer it.' Mandy slipped out into the tiny hall where the telephone was kept, and Rissa tried to quell the sudden thumping of her heart. Could it be Calum? She'd been half expecting him to ring all day, demanding to know why she had run away, but perhaps he hadn't had time. Perhaps this was the first chance he'd——

'Rissa, it's Kate.'

'Kate?'

'Yes, she's ringing from somewhere in America, I didn't catch where. Wants to know where Alison is.'

'I'd better speak to her.' Rissa spoke reluctantly, all Alison's accusations flooding back. How could she talk to Kate on the old footing with that hanging between them? She came out into the hall and took the receiver. 'Hullo, Kate.'

'Rissa, honey!' The warm American voice sounded as clear as if her stepmother was in the next room. 'It's good to hear your voice. Honey, I reckon I'll be coming over again soon, you'd never believe how homesick I've been these past weeks! How are you? How is that tea-room going along?'

'Oh, fine, fine,' Rissa answered hurriedly, thinking

how much the call must be costing. 'Kate, Mandy said you were asking about Alison——'

'Yeah, there's someone here wants to see her. Leaving right away, in fact, so I thought I'd better check up and make sure she was still around. Mandy tells me she's off on some trip, though.'

'Yes, she went to Edinburgh, with—with Calum. You remember Calum Kilmartin?' Rissa held her breath, waiting for Kate's reaction to the name. Would it tell her anything? 'I went too, but I came back early—Alison should be back tomorrow.'

'Calum Kilmartin? You mean that pianist guy she ran around with for a while?' It certainly didn't sound like the way a woman would refer to her previous lover. 'Say, is there anything going on between those two?'

'I don't know. There may be. They've seen a lot of each other.'

'Hm,' Kate said. 'Well, Calum's a nice enough guy, but I don't see him as the man for Alison. Too dedicated to his work. Okay, honey, so long as she's coming back. I'd better ring off now, I'm on a friend's phone. And just look out—I reckon I'll be back for that tea pretty soon now!'

Thoughtfully, Rissa replaced the receiver. Kate certainly hadn't reacted much to Calum's name—to her, he could have been just another man, 'nice enough' but not really interesting. Could it be true that this was how she saw him; that he had never been more than that to her?

'Someone wants to get in touch with Alison,' she reported, returning to the kitchen. 'Her agent, I'd guess. Probably got some fantastic new modelling assignment in Bermuda to offer her!'

'That would be interesting,' said Mandy. 'Seeing whether she accepts it, I mean. Did you say she's still coming back tomorrow, Rissa?'

'Yes, I did. Why?'

'Oh, I just wondered if she and Calum might extend their stay, now she's got him on her own, I mean. I should think there are plenty of his cronies in Edinburgh too just now, with the Festival just about to start.'

'Oh, I think he'll come back,' said Rissa, wishing that she could be away before he did. 'He'll be practising night and day now that it's so close.'

She moved slowly towards the window, looking out at the loch and thinking of Kate. She really *hadn't* sounded as if Calum meant any more to her than a casual acquaintance. Rissa was inclined to believe her. She *wanted* to believe her—but she still couldn't quite bring herself to believe that even Alison would have levelled such an accusation against her own mother if there hadn't been some truth in it.

And anyway that still left the first Mrs Loring, Rissa's mother, who had spent so much time with Calum when he was a young man. There was no way she could find out the truth about that. No way at all.

'Could you answer the phone, Rissa?' Mandy asked, popping her head into the kitchen. 'I've got a new crowd of customers just arrived, and I hate keeping people waiting.'

'All right.' Rissa dusted flour from her hands and went out to the hall. 'Hullo? Cluny Cottage here.'

'Oh, is that Rissa?' For a moment she thought it was Kate again, then she realised it was Alison. She felt her body freeze, but there wasn't a hint of embarrassment in Alison's tone. 'Look, honey, I'm awfully sorry to give you this trouble, but I've decided to continue my trip from here. I won't be coming back to Ichrachan. Well, I guess I've seen most of what there is to see around there, haven't I? And Mandy'll be pleased to get back in her own room.' She gave a husky laugh. 'Anyway, what I called for was to ask you if you'd pack my things up for me and send them on. I've arranged for a car to call over and collect them. Would that be asking too much?'

'No—no, it's perfectly all right.' Rissa shook her

head, trying to clear the dazed feeling. 'You mean you're not coming back at all?'

'That's right, sweetie. I'm staying on in Edinburgh for a while and then—well, I guess I haven't really made up my mind yet.' The throaty laugh sounded like doom in Rissa's ears. 'Say goodbye to all the folks for me, will you? And thanks for a good time.'

'Yes—yes, I will.' Rissa hardly knew what she was saying. 'But—the car, when will it be coming?'

'Oh, some time tomorrow. Sorry to give you this trouble, Rissa, but it really is quite important that I have the rest of my things now, you see that, don't you? Anyway, I'll have to fly now. Love to Mandy and her fisherman. 'Bye!'

' 'Bye,' Rissa answered mechanically, and after a moment she put down the receiver. She stood there, staring absently at the wall. So Alison wasn't coming back! What did it mean? Gloomily, Rissa thought she knew.

Alison and Calum must be staying in Edinburgh together. They'd come to an agreement—probably they would be getting married, soon after the Festival. And then Alison's modelling days would be at an end and she would be spending her life at Calum's side, travelling with him from engagement to engagement, sustaining him through the nerve-racking performances, the long weeks of practice.

Living the life that even now Rissa had to acknowledge was her idea of paradise.

It didn't take long to pack the clothes Alison had left behind. Rissa did it herself, refusing Mandy's offer to help, and when she had finished the room looked bare and unoccupied. It would be nice to see Mandy's cheerful jumble here, making the place seem itself again before she married Donald and they moved into the large bedroom, as Rissa had insisted they should.

She had already started to look for a job, ordering a weekly magazine that specialised in advertising such posts from the newsagent in Ichrachan. As it happened, he had one in stock; he didn't sell a lot, he explained, but usually had two or three delivered, and this one hadn't been bought. Rissa brought it home and scanned it quickly while she ate her supper. Now that the packing was finished, she would look at it more thoroughly.

There were three that had possibilities, two in hotels and one as housekeeper in a large country house in Cumbria. The husband was a writer, the wife busy with three small children, and they wanted a housekeeper to run things generally. A small flat was provided, and the successful applicant would have the use of a car, even able to take it away for holidays. The wording of the advertisement sounded friendly, and Rissa made up her mind to telephone them straightaway. If it was as nice as it sounded, it could be ideal; well away from Ichrachan yet not too far for the occasional visit. And Cumbria was a beautiful part of the country.

So why was she so reluctant to lift the phone and make that call?

The thought of Calum decided her. The next time he came to Ichrachan he would have Alison with him— almost certainly as his wife. Did she want to be here when that happened? Could she really sit by and watch the two of them together, knowing it was for life?

She lifted the phone and dialled the number in Cumbria, determined that this time there would be no turning back. She was finished with Calum Kilmartin, and he with her. This was to be the start of a new life.

The voice that answered was deep and pleasant—the writer, no doubt. Yes, he said, they were still looking for a housekeeper, although they had had several replies to their advertisement. They would be holding interviews at the end of next week, if she would like to come. She could stay the night. Yes, her qualifications sounded ideal, and she was by far the youngest of the applicants so far. It would be nice for the children to have a young housekeeper. And if she was running a tea-room she would be able to make a lot of the things his children liked best.

Rissa replaced the telephone, feeling oddly exhausted. So that was settled. And if she didn't get this job, at least she'd made a start. After this, applying would be easier. Perhaps it would be a good idea to write to those hotels too. . . .

The days passed slowly. They were busy enough—Rissa marvelled at the number of people who came to Cluny Cottage, considering that this was their first season and they had had no advertising. They were even collecting a few 'regular' customers—people who were self-catering or camping in the area and dropped in two or three times during the week, often buying cakes to take away with them. And tourists frequently called in a few days after their first visit, on their way back from the Highlands. It gave Rissa a small glow of pleasure to recognise these faces and know that they had called back specially.

There was no word of Calum. Presumably he had stayed in Edinburgh for discussions and rehearsals, Alison with him. Rissa tried hard not to think about him, but although she was generally successful during the day it proved almost impossible at night, when she lay in bed gazing out over the moonlit waters of the loch and letting her mind roam over the events that had taken place since she had returned to Cluny. She knew it was foolish; knew that she shouldn't conjure up visions of those walks she had once enjoyed with Calum, the long days sailing and swimming years ago. Even worse, the memories of the day Calum had rescued her from the storm and the night they had spent together. She moved her head restlessly on the pillow, wondering what would have happened if she had behaved differently. And that evening when he had taken her to Kilvanie—could she have changed things then by being more submissive, by letting her body take charge? It all depended, she thought wretchedly, on the truth of Alison's remarks. If Calum was indeed the womaniser she declared him, then Rissa was well out of it and would surely have ended up even more badly hurt. It was something she could never know.

She had had replies from the two hotels, one of which proved unsuitable after all, the other already interviewing several applicants; Rissa would be notified should none of the applicants be suitable. Rissa guessed that she would hear no more from them, and she searched the next copy of the magazine, picking out a few more that looked likely. But she wouldn't contact them until after Friday, when she was due to travel to Cumbria for her interview with the writer.

The last day dragged interminably. Rissa was plagued by the feeling that she was about to make an irrevocably change, something she would deeply regret. Yet what else could she do? She could stay at Cluny, of course, but that would mean facing every day the memories that tortured her. It could mean having to meet Calum when he came to Kilvanie—and it would mean meeting Alison too, seeing her with Calum, living the life Rissa longed to live. No, it *must* be right to go away. John Markham, the writer in Cumbria, had sounded pleasant, the confirming letter written by his wife friendly and welcoming. How could it be so wrong to take this chance of starting a new life?

In the evening, her packing for a brief visit done, Rissa left the cottage and wandered down to the shore. It wouldn't be her last evening here; she had agreed to stay on for the Bank Holiday week before leaving Mandy, and there was no question of her missing the wedding the following week. But somehow it felt like her last evening. From tomorrow—if she got the job—everything would be different. It was as if a part of her life was coming to an end.

The blazing heat of the day had faded to a pleasant coolness that made it just necessary to drape a light cardigan round her shoulders. The brush of air against her skin was refreshing, and she lifted her face to it as she walked along. Beyond the mouth of the loch the sea glowed apricot as the sun sank down behind the rippling waves; here, between the mountains, the water was like a mirror.

Rissa drifted slowly along the shore, barely noticing where she was going. They had heard no more from Alison, nor had they expected to. She had almost faded from their minds as if she had never been, though for Rissa she would never disappear entirely; she had caused too much pain. But it was a pain she might well have experienced even without Alison's influence, she admitted. If she had allowed Calum to take possession of her heart and her body, she could even now have been wandering along the shore, badly hurt, her self-possession and self-respect shattered.

At least she still had that. At least she had nothing to be ashamed of—but just at this moment, that was cold comfort.

Deep in her thoughts, Rissa hadn't noticed how far she was walking. She lifted her head suddenly in surprise, tilting it sideways. Was that music she could hear—the clear notes of a piano?

She realised then that she was almost at Kilvanie, within yards of the little private jetty at the end of the garden.

Oh no! She'd never meant to come this way—what could have possessed her? Even though as far as she knew Calum was still in Edinburgh, preparing for his performance next week. She had made a private vow, lying one night sleepless in Cluny Cottage, that she would never come near Kilvanie again. There was only one way to forget Calum Kilmartin, and that was to cut him and everything that reminded her of him clean out of her life.

And now here she was, on the edge of the loch, in full view of those long windows. The low white house stretched along the top of the garden, glimmering in the fading light. She wanted to go away, but she couldn't. She stared at it, fascinated. And then she heard it again—the notes of a piano, carrying softly but clearly on the cool evening air.

It was almost as if there were some magnetic force that wouldn't allow her to move away. She knew that she ought to go, back to Cluny Cottage, away from Kilvanie and this strange, almost supernatural influence the sight of the house and the sound of the music were exerting upon her. But she couldn't. She could only draw nearer, walking slowly up the lawns towards those tall windows, towards the one soft light that she could now see burning near the grand piano; towards the dark silhouette that bent over the keyboard, playing as if life itself depended on it. And Rissa knew that whatever happened to her after this, she had to stay here now. She had to have this one last glimpse of Calum, feel the strength and the power of the bond that was between them.

She drifted nearer, her blood racing in time with the music. It was a powerful theme he was playing, something quite different from the music that had come to be associated with him, and it stirred her heart. Before she was aware of it she was almost at the door; she sank down on the grass, afraid to come nearer, and leaned her head on her hand while she listened.

Then the tempo of the music changed and she recognised the rhapsody that Calum had played to her before. The music that, he said, expressed his feelings for her. The passages rang out into the night, tearing at her heart with their torment and frenzy of a love that could never be fulfilled, and she listened, bemused. Had it really been like that? Was this the truth? But how could it be anything else, her anguished heart cried as the tears rained on her head. Oh Calum, Calum, what have we done to each other?

The torment was over, the frustration eased by a passage of sweet tenderness that caught at her emotions. If only it *could* have been like that! This must be Calum's vision of what might be; the only way he could express the love in his heart. The music rose to its climax, a climax that she knew could have been matched if only she had allowed her heart and her body to overrule her mind. Calum had known it too, and at last she understood his persistence. To know that such magic could be attained, yet to be constantly frustrated! It was no wonder he had often been angry and harsh. If only she had known!

The music was softer now, almost a lullaby as if the lovers were sleeping in each other's arms. Rissa sat perfectly still, her face still buried in her hands, her palms wet with the tears that had fallen into them. It was almost dark now and she prayed that Calum—or, worse still, Alison—would not see her there. But she couldn't move; she could do nothing but sit there until her body stopped its trembling and her legs recovered their strength.

A final chord and the concerto was ended. She sensed that Calum was sitting back, temporarily drained, his black hair falling over his forehead, his face flushed with exertion. She knew that playing sapped his strength, that for a while afterwards he was almost in a daze. As she, too, was at this moment.

The moments passed. Rissa looked out across the loch at the rising moon, at the trail of silver light it left across the still water. She knew she ought to go, before it was too late. But she couldn't move.

And then three was a sound from the room behind her. She turned her head to see a dark, bulky shadow move across the room, passing in front of the lamp. Calum came to the tall, open windows and stood there, looking out.

She saw his head move until she knew that he must see her. She felt his eyes on her, sensed that he was somehow not surprised; it was almost as if this meeting had been inevitable. She saw him take a step towards her, then stop as if undecided.

His voice came to her in the darkness, low, a little uncertain. 'Rissa?'

The spell was broken. With a little cry of dismay, Rissa scrambled to her feet and ran stumblingly down the lawn to the shore. She didn't look back until she reached the jetty, expecting at every moment to feel Calum's hand descend roughly on her shoulder. But when at last she did pause, shaking, by the water's edge and allow herself to turn, there was nothing to be seen. Only the light shape of the white house in the gathering darkness and the long, empty lawn.

CHAPTER NINE

By the time Rissa reached Carlisle the next afternoon she was tired and more than ready to stop driving and rest. She was thankful that she had only another twenty miles to go, and once out of the town she pulled in to a layby and studied the directions she had been given.

Her experience last night had proved conclusively that she must get away from Ichrachan. Calum was an even greater danger to her than he had been before. His music and his presence had mesmerised her so that flight had been her only salvation. Even though Alison might have been—surely *must* have been—in the house with him, Rissa's one desire had been to go into his arms and stay there. She couldn't stay where her desires could rule her like that—she had to get away, somewhere where she could regain control.

The softer landscape of England calmed her thoughts. Here there were green fields and woods without the dramatic backdrop of the mountains at Ichrachan, or even those that would appear if she penetrated further into the Lake District. Perhaps where the countryside was quieter, her thoughts and feelings might also calm down. She hoped so, anyway; living with them as taut as violin strings was becoming too exhausting.

John Markham's house was lost in the countryside between Carlisle and Penrith. Following the directions, Rissa drove through winding lanes, passing through villages that never saw a tourist, and already she felt a kind of peace stealing into her heart. She wondered if she would be lucky enough to get this job, and what her employers would be like. She had heard of John Markham and read one or two of his books, vivid adventure stories that had managed to keep her awake,

175

reading, far into the night. He researched his books by visiting the places he wrote about, and kept his own yacht for sailing to different parts of the world. She wondered if he took his wife and children with him.

If was almost five when she finally arrived and stopped the car in the drive of the large house. She sat for a moment looking at it; a comfortable, slightly ugly, very solid-looking house. There was an air of contentment about it; somehow it reminded her of Kilvanie, though she had never seen Kilvanie radiate quite that atmosphere of goodwill unless it was in her dreams.

The front door opened and a tall, thin woman came out, followed by two small children. Rissa got out of the car and they shook hands.

'I'm Penelope Markham. I hope you had a good journey and aren't too tired. Would you like to bring your things in now?' She paused as she led Rissa into the house. 'John's working at present, but if you'd like to come down for a cup of tea he'll come and meet you. I must tell you how glad we are that you've applied for this job. All the other applicants have been in their fifties, and with three children we really do feel that someone younger would be better.'

Rissa followed her up the stairs. She felt slightly unreal, as if she was dreaming. She seemed to have no control over events now, although she had made her own decision to apply for this job and had come quite happily for the interview. What was wrong with her? Penelope Markham seemed a pleasant enough woman and was making her welcome. So why this sudden feeling of apprehension?

The room was comfortable, with a good view, and Rissa was left to wash. Feeling sticky in the clothes she had been driving in, she changed into a cool linen dress in pale cream, and brushed her honey-coloured hair. She looked competent and sensible enough in the mirror, anyway; she wondered wryly what her prospective employers would think if they could see into the turmoil that lay under that cool exterior.

However, neither Penelope Markham nor her husband appeared to notice anything unusual as they gave Rissa tea on the terrace, overlooking a pleasant garden. They chatted easily, asking her about her journey and then going on to the subject of Ichrachan, obviously curious as to why she was leaving her home. Rissa explained that her sister was getting married and staying there, and this seemed a good opportunity to branch out, and she was thankful to see that they accepted this.

The children arrived home just as they were finishing their tea. They came on to the terrace and shook hands with Rissa, their eyes wide and curious. Rissa smiled back at them and thought how lucky John and Penelope Markham were. This lovely, peaceful home, an interesting life and three children—what more could anyone ask? And a pang went through her as she thought of what might have been—herself and Calum, turning Kilvanie into just such a haven that they could return to between his engagements, and filling it with the noise and laughter of just such a family. . . . But it wouldn't be herself and Calum—it would be Calum and Alison. And whether they would make of Kilvanie the home that she dreamed of remained very much to be seen.

Rissa shook herself crossly. She had come here to forget Kilvanie and Calum Kilmartin, hadn't she? And she had even begun to succeed. Surely these children, their small hands already tugging at her as they demanded to be allowed to show her the garden, would help more than anything else.

'Leave Miss Loring alone, Lucy,' Penelope Markham ordered. 'She's tired after her long drive.'

'No, I'd like to see the garden.' Rissa got up and Lucy gave her mother a triumphant glance. 'Is there a pond? Do you have tadpoles?'

'Yes, but not now, they're frogs. Jonathan fell in once and they got all in his clothes.' Lucy kept a firm hold on Rissa's hand as they led her away across the lawn.

'Rebecca doesn't like tadpoles. She'd rather have the goldfish pond.' There was scorn in the young voice and Rissa smiled down at the shy Rebecca. 'Jonathan and me like the tadpole pond best.'

'Which do you like?' Jonathan asked in an unexpectedly deep voice, and three pairs of eyes stared at her anxiously.

It was almost like a test of character, Rissa thought in amusement, and answered diplomatically, 'I like them both about the same, I think. It depends what sort of mood I'm in.' And this was evidently a satisfactory answer to all three, for there was a definite relaxing in their manner as they plunged into the shadow of the trees surrounding the wide lawn and made for the wild part of the garden that was their own especial domain.

It was there that they were found some time later by John Markham, sitting in a circle on the grass while Rissa told them stories. He stood looking down at them for a while before they noticed him; then Lucy gave an exclamation of delight and Rissa glanced up and then hastily scrambled to her feet.

'Oh dear, I'm all covered in twigs,' she said, brushing them from her skirt. 'I'm sorry, did you wonder where we'd got to? I'm afraid I forget about time.'

'No need to worry,' he smiled. 'Penelope and I thought you might need rescuing, that's all. These savages will do anything to escape bedtime.'

'Oh, it's *not* bedtime!' Lucy protested. 'We haven't had any supper yet, and we haven't finished our story——'

'You've had more than enough stories, if I know you.' John Markham lifted Lucy and Jonathan to their feet with one movement. 'Get along in with you. Your supper's ready and waiting.'

'Will Rissa come and say goodnight to us?'

'Yes, of course I will,' she promised, and the children turned away, still reluctantly, but a moment or two later were racing each other across the lawn, Lucy screaming frightful threats as to what would happen to the one who reached the terrace last.

John Markham turned to Rissa and grinned ruefully. 'Hope that hasn't put you off coming here,' he remarked as they walked slowly through the garden. 'I'm afraid they're a bit wild at times.'

'They're lovely children,' Rissa said impulsively. 'I'll love being here—that's if you think I'm suitable.'

'Oh, there's no question of that.' He held out his hand and Rissa shook it, feeling warmth flood through her as she allowed herself to realise that this was to be her home, at least for a while, that here she would be able to regain peace of mind, acquire the contentment and serenity that seemed to be part of the place. Here she could forget Calum; forget the *Tormented Rhapsody* that had such power to reduce her to the tears of a broken heart; close her heart to an episode of her life that was, she suspected, always going to be too painful to remember.

Here, with John and Penelope Markham and their three lively children, she could begin to build her life anew. Find the old Rissa. Or—better still, perhaps— discover a new one.

John took her back slowly through the garden, though he admitted that his wife would have made a better guide. 'She's the one who looks after all this,' he said, waving a hand. 'Spends hours grubbing about among the weeds. When we came here it was nothing more than a jungle.'

'It's beautiful now.' Rissa was beginning to relax and feel that she could be happy here. Ichrachan already seemed a long way from this peaceful spot; surely here she could begin to find herself again. 'Isn't that your wife waving on the terrace? It look as if she wants you.'

They turned back. 'Oh, it's the phone,' said John Markham, evidently understanding the kind of home-spun semaphore his wife was using. 'But I think it's you she wants, my dear. Odd—I hope there's nothing happened at your home.'

Rissa broke into a run, but before she reached the terrace she could see that Penelope Markham was shaking her head.

'Don't rush—he's gone now. It was a friend of yours,' she went on as Rissa came nearer. 'Said he was passing close by and had an important message to deliver. He's staying to dinner.' She turned to her husband, smiling. 'It's someone you'll be interested to meet, too,' she added. 'Calum Kilmartin, the pianist.'

Rissa saw Calum's car arrive as she was getting ready for dinner. She looked out of the window, her heart doing its usual trick of trying to choke her. Why had he followed her here? What could Mandy have been thinking of, telling him where she was? Why couldn't he just leave her alone?

She had been unable to say anything to the Markhams, who were evidently delighted with their unexpected guest. What could she say, anyway? It was too late to put Calum off, and she doubted whether it would have been possible. He was evidently determined to continue pursuing her, though what good it would do was beyond her understanding. And what was Alison's view of it all?

Well, there was nothing for it but to put a brave face on it and carry the situation off with as much aplomb as she could gather around her. At least he couldn't do or say much with the Markhams present, and she would make very sure that he didn't get a chance to be alone with her. She would even, if he showed signs of overstaying his welcome, plead tiredness and go to bed early. Rude or not, she wasn't going to take any more risks where Calum was concerned.

However, she was glad that she had brought her favourite dress to wear for dinner—a low-necked lacy affair in delphinium blue. Her topaz eyes were shadowed and she touched them up with amethyst to hide the weariness. A dash of lipstick and a dab of a favourite perfume that Mandy had given her for her birthday, and she was ready.

Or, at least, as ready as she would ever be.

Calum was in the big, slightly untidy, drawing-room, a whisky and soda in his hand, chatting easily with his hosts when Rissa arrived. The children had all been put to bed and Penelope Markham had changed into a green caftan that suited her tall slender figure. They turned as Rissa came in, and to her dismay Calum came straight over and took her in his arms.

'Calum!' she whispered in entreaty, but he ignored her pleading eyes and laid his lips on hers in a kiss that left her flushed and angry. She glanced quickly at the Markhams and was even more discomfited to see that they were both smiling. What on earth had Calum been telling them?

Whatever it was, there was no further hint of it and the conversation was general as they went in to dinner. Rissa ate her roast lamb and apple crumble almost without noticing it, waiting all the time for Calum to embarrass her again. But he didn't, and she was relieved to find herself having to say very little. John and Penelope Markham were both obviously fans of Calum and had actually been to some of his concerts, and they were more than happy to allow him to monopolise the conversation. In fact, it was the kind of conversation that at any other time would have held Rissa spellbound. Tonight, however, she scarcely heard a word.

'You really will?' Penelope Markham exclaimed as they went back to the drawing-room for coffee. 'But that's a tremendous honour! To hear the new concerto, before its first public performance! But are you sure you want to?'

Calum smiled and went over to the piano, while Rissa watched him with agonised eyes. No, she wanted to scream. To hear *Tormented Rhapsody* again, with all it meant, here in this unfamiliar room with these people who, however kind, were essentially strangers—it was too cruel. She glanced at Mrs Markham, wondering if she could make an excuse and slip away, but before she could speak Calum had forestalled her.

'I'll have to ask Rissa to manage the score for me,' he said, and she glowered at him, knowing that he needed no such help and anyway she wasn't at all able to give it. 'I've got it with me—like taking your harp to a party, isn't it?—but it's in such a mess, all loose sheets, you know.' He turned his steel-bright gaze on Rissa, daring her to refuse. 'Come out to the car with me and I'll fetch it.'

'And you really must stay the night,' Penelope interposed. 'We can't turn you out into the darkness when you've given us such a treat. Unless you've somewhere already booked?'

'No, I haven't, as a matter of fact.' Calum smiled charmingly at her. 'It's very kind of you, I'd love to stay. Coming, Rissa?'

Seething, Rissa followed him. Well, he couldn't do much to her in front of the house in broad daylight— well, twilight, anyway. 'Calum, what are you playing at?' she hissed as soon as they were outside the door. 'What are you doing here? What did you tell them, for heaven's sake?'

'Why, that you and I were engaged to be married and you'd applied for the job after a misunderstanding,' he replied calmly. 'It's all right, Rissa, they understand the situation perfectly. They took it very well—disappointed, of course, that they won't be enjoying your home-made bread and treacle tart, but they'll be brave about that. May I say how very pretty you're looking, especially with your eyes flashing like that. They remind me——'

Rissa found her voice at last. 'Remind you?' she raged. 'I don't care *what* they remind you of! So far as I'm concerned I wish you'd forget me, Calum, just as I've been trying to forget you. What's the *point* of all this? It's never going to work, haven't you realised that yet? And how dare you tell them all those lies? Do you realise you've lost me a good job, a job I'd have enjoyed? And as for understanding the situation perfectly, I just don't see how they can—*I* certainly can't!'

'But then you never have, have you?' he said softly.
'A state of affairs which I intend to put right very soon,
before this night's over, in fact. Nice of the Markhams
to ask me to stay, isn't it? Especially after I've virtually
stolen their new housekeeper from under their noses.
It'll enable us to have a good long talk, without fear of
interruption.'

'That's what you think! I'm not talking to you here
or anywhere else, and there's no way you can force me.
And as for stealing me from the Markhams, that's
easily put right. I'll just tell them you're a raving lunatic
and have been pestering me for the last three months,
and ask them to send for your attendant to come and
collect you! I've no doubt Alistair would oblige, if I
asked him.'

'I've no doubt of that either,' Calum murmured, his
voice menacing. 'But you won't try it, Rissa. You'll
listen to me. And believe me, I *could* force you to do so,
quite easily.' His hand came up to her face and touched
her cheek with a caress that sent fire through her limbs.
'As you very well know.'

A shudder ran through Rissa. She turned stiffly and
followed Calum back into the house. Nothing could
matter now; there was nothing she could do to alter the
course of events. Whatever Calum wanted to do, he
would do it. And he called *her* spoilt!

It was evident that Calum had no intention of letting
Rissa slip away from him again. He positioned her by
the piano, showing her the score; he knew as well as she
did that she wouldn't have the faintest idea of when a
page would need turning and would have to turn them
at random. She also knew that it wouldn't make the
slightest difference; Calum didn't need the score to play
this concerto. She glanced at the Markhams and they
were smiling, half indulgently and half with anticipation.
Well, it would be an experience for them to recount to
their friends, she thought dully. They probably thought
they were getting good value from their two guests.

Calum started to play. Rissa had steeled herself for

this moment, determined not to let it affect her as it had
before. After all, they weren't at Kilvanie with the
moon tracing a silvery path across the loch and the
mountains rearing all around. They were in an alien
drawing-room, with two strangers watching and
listening. . . . But it was no use. The first chords caught
at her heart, wrenching at the emotions she had tried so
hard to bury. She listened in a trance, forgetting to turn
the score sheets, hearing only the plaintive notes that
called an echo from her own soul. The torment of
frustration and impossible love surged around her, the
piano sobbing out its desire as she had so often sobbed
into her pillow. Her knuckles whitened as she pressed
her hands down on the piano; her eyes filled with tears.
She was aware of nothing, nothing but the music which
had come straight from Calum's heart to hers. There
was a chair close to her, and at last she abandoned all
pretence and sank into it, burying her face in her hands.

The tender passage followed, but its sweetness only
brought fresh tears, and she knew that she had been on
the point of throwing away something infinitely
precious, something she would never find again. She
thought of the expression in Calum's eyes at the times
when they had been closest and knew that she had been
wrong ever to doubt him; she was filled with an
agonising fear that now it was too late.

When the music finished at last Rissa did not move.
Slowly she came back to reality; slowly she remembered
just where she was. She raised her head and looked
around the room, and found that she and Calum were
alone.

He was still sitting at the piano, watching her. His
face was grave.

'Where—where are the Markhams?' Rissa whispered.

'They slipped out some time ago. I don't think they'll
be back.' He reached out a hand. 'Come to me, Rissa.'

It was a command that meant far more than her
immediate reaction. Hesitantly, she straightened herself;
realised that once she had taken Calum's hand there

would be no turning back, realised too that he would not come to her—he had made his move, his declaration in following her here, and she had given him no reason to suppose that he had been welcome. It was up to her now.

She stood up and moved across to him. She took his hand and stood looking down into his face, feeling the shivers run like great shocks through her body. When he pulled her gently on to his knees, she went to him like a child, and gave a great, shuddering sigh as he cradled her at last in his warm, strong arms.

'And now,' he murmured into her ear, his lips brushing the soft lobe, 'let's have that talk we've been promising ourselves.'

'You said once that speech got in the way,' Rissa whispered. 'You said there were better ways of communicating. . . .'

'And so there are, you brazen hussy.' His voice was soft with sudden amusement. 'But there are some things that have to be sorted out with speech. And they have to be sorted out first—unfortunately. Now, why don't we move over to that sofa, which looks rather more comfortable than this piano stool, and get down to business.'

Still dazed, Rissa allowed him to carry her to the sofa, her heart racing as she remembered the last time Calum had done such a thing. But he didn't kneel beside her and caress her as he'd done at Kilvanie; he sat down, pulling her into his arms, and gave her a tender, almost passionless, kiss before he began to speak.

'Now then. You first, or me?'

'It had better be you,' Rissa said, still hardly able to believe what was happening. 'I don't know where to start. Except——' she stared at him, a frown gathering her brows together '—what happened about Alison? Aren't you getting married after all?'

'Married? To Alison?' Calum gave a great shout of laughter. 'Rissa, you can't have ever seriously believed

that I'd want to do such a thing? Look, I had Alison up
to here years ago. I know all the pretty little tricks that
one can pull, believe me! Marry her? I feel pity for the
poor devil who's taken her on!'

'Taken her on? You mean—Calum, what *do* you
mean?' she asked helplessly. 'Look, start at the
beginning. Explain everything you've just said. Because
none of it makes any sense at all to me.'

Calum stopped laughing. 'Yes, you really do look
bewildered. Poor Rissa, have you been very confused?
Well, you had me pretty baffled too at times, I may tell
you. And there were others when I could cheerfully
have strangled you. Now, what do you want me to
explain?'

'Well, since we're doing some sorting out, why not go
right back to the beginning? You said you'd had
enough of Alison years ago. Just what did happen that
time, Calum? I heard Alison's version.'

'And that was?'

For the first time, Rissa couldn't meet his eyes.
'She—she said you'd been having an affair with Kate.'

'I see.' His voice was grim. 'Well, I thought I was up
to all her tricks, like I said, but I hadn't thought of that
one. No, I never had an affair with Kate, Rissa. She
wasn't interested in me, only in your father. And I
wasn't interested in her—not in that way. But I admit
that Alison did have me interested for a while—and I
was happy to have it that way, until she started to press
me about marriage.'

'You didn't want to marry her, then?' Rissa asked,
and he shook his head firmly.

'Not then, nor any other time. Oh, I know I was
wrong to take what she offered—but she'd spun me this
line about being free and liberated, no strings and all
that—and I swallowed it. Not for long—the attraction
soon wore thin when I realised what she was really
like—but long enough for her to spin me another line;
that she was pregnant.' He stopped, his eyes hard. 'I
knew there was no way *that* could be true, and I made it

clear that it was all off between us. Alison raged and
stormed, but she had to take it. I never saw her again
until she arrived at Cluny the other week, and I never
wanted to.' His eyes had softened again as he looked
down at Rissa. 'I owe you one hell of an apology over
this,' he said quietly. 'I'd give anything for that earlier
episode not to have happened, and I shouldn't have
used Alison to make you jealous. But I just couldn't see
any other way of getting through to you. And even that
was my own fault—if I hadn't been such a swine that
first time we met, it would have been a lot easier. But
after Alison I'd never really trusted another woman,
you see. I'd never let one get to my heart again. And the
way you made me feel when I saw you standing there—
well, it scared me! I was no longer in control, and I
didn't like that.'

'It scared me, too,' Rissa said simply. 'I couldn't
understand what was happening. But—did you say
something about someone *taking Alison* on? What did
you mean? I thought, when she rang to say she was
staying in Edinburgh, that it was you——'

'Not on your life! You know, I must send that guy
the biggest crate of malt whisky they make. Talk about
being saved from a fate worse than death! I didn't
discover you'd gone from the hotel until next morning,
you know—Alison waited up to give me the good news,
but I was so late even she had to give in and go to bed.
Next day she told me that you'd run away with
Alistair—nothing about his course or the fact that he'd
actually taken you home, of course—just let me believe
that you'd eloped together. Well, I nearly went crazy. I
didn't have time to do anything about it that day, but
once I got clear in the evening I started trying to trace
him. All they knew in Glasgow was that he was in
Edinburgh, nobody seemed to have any idea exactly
where, on some course. So I had to track that down,
and by the time I finally did he'd gone back to his digs.
I had a devil of a job to find out where they were, and
then his landlady turned out to be all protective and

told me he was asleep and mustn't be disturbed, he'd been up all night the night before. I had to practically feign death before she'd call him, and when she did he wasn't at all keen to tell me where you were. So then I had to persuade him that I wasn't playing fast and loose. By the time we got that sorted out it was too late to do anything else, and I'd had nearly enough anyway. I still couldn't understand why you'd taken off like that. So I just shrugged my shoulders and tried to tell myself it was good riddance. And, naturally, Alison was waiting to fill the gap.'

Naturally. Rissa felt cold. Her eyes asked him the questions her lips dared not frame, and he smiled and shook his head.

'No, we didn't. But only because I was too damned tired! I think if I hadn't been I'd have said what the hell and taken whatever she cared to give. And then I'd have been in an even worse mess, wouldn't I! But luck was with me. By the morning, Alison was a different girl. She'd had this transatlantic telephone call. This Maxwell character—her boy-friend, I gathered—had found out where she was and booked himself on Concorde to arrive some time that day! Well, I was completely forgotten from then on. I never saw a girl move so fast! New clothes—hairdresser—facial, manicure, the lot. And out of my nice, friendly, shabby hotel into a smart new one where a traveller on Concorde wouldn't be ashamed to stay. I never saw her after that—never saw him, either.' He held Rissa a little tighter. 'But it didn't cheer me up all that much, though I was thankful for my escape. I still didn't have you—and all I could think of was you really didn't love me at all. That what I thought I'd seen in your eyes was after all simply chemistry, and you'd decided it wasn't enough.'

'No, I loved you all the time,' Rissa told him frankly. 'It was you who dragged chemistry into it.'

'That was when I still didn't want to admit the truth,' he said ruefully. 'God, what a fool I was, Rissa! Can you ever forgive me?'

'I already have,' she whispered. 'So long as you've forgiven me. . . . But why did you follow me here, then?'

'You came to Kilvanie last night, remember? I was playing the Rhapsody and you came and sat just outside, listening. I knew then that I had to try again—that I had to keep on and on trying, until at last I succeeded. You ran away from me then and I didn't try to follow you—from previous experience I knew that things could so easily go wrong again. But this morning I went to Cluny and saw Mandy. She told me where you were—told me a lot of other things, too. She has quite a forceful tongue, your young sister.'

'I know. I've experienced it myself.'

'Well, I decided that I had to follow you. I couldn't let you go to strangers without at least one more try. So—here I am.'

Rissa reached her arms around her his neck and drew his head down to hers. Here he was. Close in her arms, her face against his, with no secrets between them any more.

She didn't need to ask that last question. Alison's accusation about Rissa's mother had been as false as everything else she had said. She had never believed it—only been so shocked and horrified that she had had to run away rather than face Calum with even the slightest suspicion. But there was no need for that now.

Calum's kiss deepened suddenly, driving all thought from her mind, and now she found herself able at last to give herself up, totally and joyfully, to his embrace. His hand slid down her neck, into the deep slash between her breasts, and she sighed and moved closer, knowing that now there would be no holding back, no fears and no inhibitions.

'I've just thought,' Calum murmured against her lips. 'The Markhams asked me to stay the night—but I've no idea where my room is.'

'It doesn't matter,' Rissa whispered back. 'Share mine. I'm sure they won't mind.'

'We'll send them an invitation to the wedding,' he said, and drew her to her feet.

And they went slowly up the stairs together, arms twined about each other. It might be unconventional, Rissa thought as they closed the bedroom door behind them and came again into each other's arms, but something Alison had said was true, at least. Artists were known to be unconventional, weren't they?

And as Calum made love to her through the long, moonlit night, she gave constant and heartfelt thanks that it should be so.

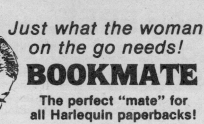
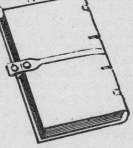

Yours FREE, with a home subscription to HARLEQUIN SUPERROMANCE.™

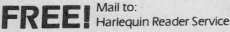

Complete and mail
the coupon below today!

FREE!

Mail to:
Harlequin Reader Service

In the U.S.
2504 West Southern Avenue
Tempe, AZ 85282

In Canada
P.O. Box 2800, Postal Station "A"
5170 Yonge St., Willowdale, Ont. M2N 5T5

YES, please send me FREE and without any obligation my
HARLEQUIN SUPERROMANCE novel, LOVE BEYOND DESIRE. If you do
not hear from me after I have examined my FREE book, please send me
the 4 new **HARLEQUIN SUPERROMANCE** books every month as soon
as they come off the press. I understand that I will be billed only $2.50 for
each book (total $10.00). There are no shipping and handling or any
other hidden charges. There is no minimum number of books that I have
to purchase. In fact, I may cancel this arrangement at any time.
LOVE BEYOND DESIRE is mine to keep as a FREE gift, even if I do not
buy any additional books.   134 BPS KAP2

NAME _____ (Please Print)

ADDRESS _____ APT. NO. _____

CITY _____

STATE/PROV. _____ ZIP/POSTAL CODE _____

SIGNATURE (If under 18, parent or guardian must sign.)

SUP-SUB-11

This offer is limited to one order per household and not valid to present
subscribers. Prices subject to change without notice.
Offer expires January 31, 1985

Dear Reader

With the aim of giving a maximum amount of information in a limited number of pages Michelin has adopted a system of symbols which is today known the world over.

Failing this system the present publication would run to six volumes.

Judge for yourselves by comparing the descriptive text below with the equivalent extract from the Guide in symbol form.

🏠 ✿✿ **Cheval Blanc** (Durand) Ⓜ ⤦, ✆ 28 31 42, ≼ lake, 🏛 « garden » — 🛏wc 🚿 🐕 🚗. 🆎
closed December and Wednesday — **M** 80/145 st — ⛌ 22 — **32 rm** 145/210
Spec. Ris de veau à la crème, Poularde bressanne, tarte flambée. **Wines.** Viré, Morgon.

A comfortable hotel where you will enjoy a pleasant stay and be tempted to prolong your visit.

The excellence of the cuisine, which is personally supervised by the proprietor Mr Durand, is worth a detour.

The hotel in its quiet secluded setting away from the built-up-area offers every modern amenity.

To reserve phone 28 31 42.

The hotel affords a fine view of the lake ; in good weather it is possible to eat out of doors. The hotel is enhanced by an attractive garden.

Bedrooms with private bathroom with toilet or private shower without toilet. Telephone in room.

Parking facilities, under cover, are available to all guests with this Guide.

The hotel accepts payment by American Express credit cards.

The establishment is closed throughout December and every Wednesday.

Prices : st = service is included in all prices. There should be no supplementary charge for service, taxes or VAT on your bill.

The set meal prices range from 80 F for the lowest to 145 F for the highest.

The cost of continental breakfast served in the bedroom is 22 F.

32 bedroomed hotel. The charges vary from 145 F for a single to 210 F for the best twin bedded room.

Included for the gourmet are some culinary specialities, recommended by the hotelier : Ris de veau à la crème, Poularde bressanne, tarte flambée. In addition to the best quality wines you will find many of the local wines worth sampling : Viré, Morgon.

This demonstration clearly shows that each entry contains a great deal of information. The symbols are easily learnt and to know them will enable you to understand the Guide and to choose those establishments that you require.

CONTENTS